ADVENTURES OF JAZZI G

SEARCH FOR THE
MISSING PEACE

Advance Praise for
SEARCH FOR THE MISSING PEACE

Once in a great while, something appears in front of you that makes you stop and ask the interesting questions of life. What are we doing here? What is our purpose? Are we going to make a difference to someone? Will we leave a footprint? Will that footprint be a worthy one?

I recently had the pleasure of meeting a woman who clearly will make a difference. Her name is Gayle Johnston, and she will make a difference in a lot of readers' lives. Her book, *Search for the Missing Peace*, is a feast for the heart and soul.

—**Linda Gray**, award-winning actress, director/producer, Goodwill Ambassador to the United Nations

Through the years I have reported on some of the world's most intriguing stories: the war in Iraq, the 2004 presidential campaign, and the global war on terror, to name a few. All of these stories share a common bond in that there is a tremendous outcry for peace and security. This theme of man's hunger for peace is consistent with Gayle Johnston's wonderful story.

In *Search for the Missing Peace*, the first book in the Adventures of Jazzi G series, Gayle weaves a wonderful tale that captures a child's imagination and vision for changing the world. It is a story with a timely message: that children can have an impact on the world we live in!

—**Kelly Wright**, anchor and reporter, FOX News Channel

Jazzi G is a relatable character, and her story is a personal journey for readers as they travel with Jazzi on her own quest. *Search for the Missing Peace* will keep readers anticipating each new fantasy adventure—adventures that are both astonishing and refreshing. It is truly a magical journey, and one that supports an important message for all generations to come.

—**Joanne C. Hemingway**, My Favorite Teacher award recipient, NRRW-California, San Bernardino County Teacher of Excellence children's author

Dear Shareen,

Hope you enjoy
the search for peace!

In Christ, Love,
Gayle

ADVENTURES OF JAZZI G

SEARCH FOR THE
MISSING PEACE

GAYLE JOHNSTON

New York

ADVENTURES OF JAZZI G
SEARCH FOR THE MISSING PEACE

This is a work of fiction. Names, characters, businesses, places, events, and incidents are either the products of the author's imagination or used in a fictitious manner. Any resemblance to actual persons, living or dead, or actual events is purely coincidental.

Published in New York, New York, by Morgan James Publishing. Morgan James and The Entrepreneurial Publisher are trademarks of Morgan James, LLC.
www.MorganJamesPublishing.com

The Morgan James Speakers Group can bring authors to your live event. For more information or to book an event visit The Morgan James Speakers Group at www.TheMorganJamesSpeakersGroup.com.

Shelfie

A **free** eBook edition is available with the purchase of this print book.

CLEARLY PRINT YOUR NAME ABOVE IN UPPER CASE

Instructions to claim your free eBook edition:
1. Download the Shelfie app for Android or iOS
2. Write your name in **UPPER CASE** above
3. Use the Shelfie app to submit a photo
4. Download your eBook to any device

ISBN 978-1-63047-840-7 paperback
ISBN 978-1-63047-842-1 eBook
ISBN 978-1-63047-841-4   hardcover
Library of Congress Control Number:
2015917343

Interior Illustrations by:
Gayle Johnston

Cover Illustration by:
Gayle Johnston

Cover Design by:
Megan James

Interior Design by:
Bonnie Bushman
The Whole Caboodle Graphic Design

In an effort to support local communities and raise awareness and funds, Morgan James Publishing donates a percentage of all book sales for the life of each book to Habitat for Humanity Peninsula and Greater Williamsburg.

Get involved today, visit
www.MorganJamesBuilds.com

Habitat for Humanity
Peninsula and
Greater Williamsburg
Building Partner

In memory of my mother, the original Ginger B

CONTENTS

Chapter 1   Peace Smeech   1
Chapter 2   The Oxford Files   9
Chapter 3   A Startling Development   14
Chapter 4   Looking For Peace In All The Wrong Places   20
Chapter 5   Stuck In The Muck   25
Chapter 6   Su and Cat-Man-Doo   30
Chapter 7   Cyber-*What*?   34
Chapter 8   Living On The Edge   38
Chapter 9   Step This Way   44
Chapter 10   Just Imagine   50
Chapter 11   Rat-Whack-A-Rama   57
Chapter 12   Just When You Least Expect It!   63
Chapter 13   Iceberg Wedgie   68
Chapter 14   The Sole Man   74
Chapter 15   Lurking In The Tulips   81

Chapter 16	Ojitos Banditos	89
Chapter 17	Hot Tamales!	99
Chapter 18	The Color Of Shadows	107
Chapter 19	Frozen With Fear	113
Chapter 20	A Puddle Of Fear	122
Chapter 21	Save Da Whale, Mon	133
Chapter 22	A Kid's Caboose	143
Chapter 23	The Whine of Revenge	148
Chapter 24	Wail Of Agony	155
Chapter 25	War On Wedgies	160
Chapter 26	Where's The Peace?	165
Chapter 27	House of Peace?	172
Chapter 28	Flashback to Reality	179
	Three Weeks Later	187
	A Special Thanks	189
	About the Author	191

CHAPTER 1
PEACE SMEECH

A midst the quietness one sound remained. With head facedown, buried beneath a waterfall of strawberry blonde curls, twelve-year-old Jazzi muttered through a flurry of snorts and indiscernible babbling. Clinging to her desk as if her life depended upon it, the unsuspecting student awakened to an explosion of laughter. Mortified, her eyes darted to the safety of a nearby window.

"ALL EYES ON THE BOARD!" Mr. Shawnly shouted from the back of the classroom. Students immediately buried their cell phones, turned their eyes and bodies forward, and ceased all conversation.

Jazzi attended a private middle school located just north of San Diego, California. Perched high on a cliff, surrounded by a forest of windblown Torrey pines, it had an incredible view of the dazzling Pacific Ocean. It was a magical spot—a place where sky, land, and water joined together like old friends. But that afternoon Jazzi's thoughts weren't focused on the scenery outside her classroom window.

It was the Friday before spring vacation, and all that day she had had just one thing on her mind: freedom. One last blast from that obnoxious three o'clock bell and her dreams would come true. But now, fantasies of lazy sun-drenched afternoons came to a screeching halt.

A homework assignment on peace, and over spring break? Jazzi stared at the board in mute horror. *What teacher could be so cruel to assign homework over that most holy of all weeks? And what do I know about peace? Ever since Dad left home my life's been anything but peaceful!*

"Listen up!" The tone in Mr. Shawnly's voice was unusually serious. He paced nervously back and forth across the room, his fists clenched tightly behind his back. "A rare fever has invaded our campus." Everyone gasped. "All teachers are on high alert and ready to take action." He pulled a wadded-up handkerchief from his back pocket and wiped the beads of sweat threatening to roll down his cheeks and stain his favorite Hawaiian-print shirt.

Clouds of uneasiness hung in the air as students prepared for the worst. "Oh," he said, a mischievous grin spreading across his face. "Did I forget to mention...it's *vacation* fever?" His blue eyes twinkled.

The students groaned and collectively rolled their eyes. Whatever else you might think about him, their teacher certainly wasn't dull.

"Mr. Shawnly, MR. SHAWNLY!" Jazzi frantically waved her hands in the air.

"Question?" Mr. Shawnly sauntered over to Jazzi's desk.

"Yup!" She crossed her arms and flopped back in her seat, perturbed. "What's an assignment on peace got to do with anything?"

"Well, that's what you've got to figure out." He looked at her, amused. She stared back blankly.

"C'mon, Jazzi, you mean to tell me you never think about peace?"

"No," she huffed, "why would I? I have more important things to do."

"Ah." He tapped his finger on his chin. "I see."

Jazzi let out a disgusted sigh.

Mr. Shawnly chuckled to himself. "Perhaps you'll reconsider thinking about it over spring vacation." He lightly thumped his pencil on top of her head. "Since it's 50 percent of your final grade."

"WHAT?" Jazzi's eyes nearly popped out of her head. "That's not fair!"

"I'm sorry—*what's* not fair?"

"The peace assignment! It could take up the whole entire spring break!"

"Yes," her teacher agreed, "so be wise with your time. I'll be watching you." He stuck his pencil behind his ear and did a quick shuffle-step-kick toward his desk, all the while singing over and over, "I've got the fever…you've got the fever…" Jazzi found his off-key performance quite annoying.

Minutes later, the bell let out a high-pitched shrill that echoed through the halls. Students sprang from their desks—free at last! Only Jazzi remained sitting, dismayed by the task in front of her.

"I'll be watching you," she mimicked him sarcastically under her breath. "Peace smeech, how am I supposed to figure it out in nine days?"

Jazzi glared one last time at the homework assignment scrawled across the board, grabbed her belongings, and pouted all the way out the classroom door. With elbows bent and thumbs hooked under the straps of her backpack, she lowered her head and reluctantly plopped one foot in front of the other, moping her way westward across the schoolyard in the direction of the only peace she knew—the shore of the Pacific.

She was only a few minutes into her walk when she heard the faint sounds of kids yelling, laughing, taunting, and moving about in tight twisting fits. As the sounds grew louder she looked up from the fix of her downward gaze and realized she had happened upon a confrontation of the worst kind, one that only defines peace through defying it so bluntly—a FIGHT!

Jazzi rubbed her eyes and inched closer in to get a better view. She couldn't believe what she saw. A gawky knock-kneed kid with a knot of messed-up red hair and limbs resembling that of a baby tree flailed gracefully through the air. She stared horrified as the pale, freckle-faced boy was tossed to and fro by an unwelcomed barrage of overpowering bullies. He yelped and squealed and struck back with his sticklike arms, refusing to give up his self-respect without a fight.

Jazzi had to act fast! As far as she could tell, the only reason these self-proclaimed cool guys were bullying this poor kid was because he looked *different*. She scoured the grounds for someone to help, but there wasn't a soul in sight—it was up to her.

"HEY!" Jazzi screamed at the top of her lungs.

"Huh?" The leader turned around and looked at her. "Got a problem?"

"Actually I do!" Jazzi mustered up what little courage she had, took a deep breath, and threw down her backpack. With tightly clenched fists she pushed her way through the circle of bullies and marched straight over to the hurt boy lying on the ground. She carefully stepped over his limp body with one foot and, with the other, assumed a straddling position. With both hands planted firmly on her hips she looked directly into the leader's eyes. "You're going to have to go through *me* if you want *him*!"

"Oh no!" the leader sniveled, pretending to be scared. "Somebody help me!" He glanced around, smirking. He figured his partners in crime had his back, but rather than sticking by his side, they threw up their arms and started backing away.

"C'mon, let him go, dude," one of the boys yelled. "He's messed up enough!"

"Yeah," another one chimed in. "I say we get out of here before a teacher finds us. Besides," he added with a wink at Jazzi, "I don't want any rumors getting out that I beat up a girl."

"Wise call." Jazzi stared back defiantly.

"Hey, aren't you the chick that stroked out at your desk today in Mr. Shawnly's class?"

Jazzi's face turned instantly red. "This isn't about me!" she snapped.

The leader begrudgingly scooped up his gear and walked over to Jazzi. He got within inches of her face, snarling with an angry vengeance. "To be continued!" The fumes from his foul breath made her want to throw up.

Jazzi stood her ground as she watched the bullies bolt off in different directions. Not a trace of evidence was left behind, other than a kid curled up in the fetal position with a bloody nose and an assortment of cuts and bruises.

Jazzi knelt down beside the boy and pulled out a wadded-up napkin she had stuffed in her side pocket. "Here, use this."

He gratefully took the napkin, recognizing a familiar smell as he blotted his bloody nose. "Tacos?"

"Lunch." She stretched out her hand to help him to his feet. "You good to go?"

Embarrassed and a bit wobbly, he leaned over and picked up his glasses. "I'll live."

"Nice. I'm Jazzi, do you need me to call someone to come get you?"

"Nope, I'm good." He looked around to make sure it was safe before wiping his eyes on his ripped shirt sleeve.

"Um—name?" She gave a sly grin.

"Oh, sorry. Oxford—my name is Oxford." His swollen lips parted, attempting a smile.

"Oxford?" Jazzi hesitated. "Seriously?"

"That's my name," he said with a nod.

"That sucks." She thought a minute. "Umm—what if I call you Oxy, instead?"

"Why not?" Oxford shrugged, his head still spinning. He couldn't care less what anyone called him right now—he was just grateful his limbs were still attached.

"Yeah—Oxy—I like it!" She flung her bag over one shoulder. "So guess I'll see ya around school sometime—Oxy."

Oxford stared in awe as Jazzi strutted past him. He could only imagine how good it must feel to know you had practically saved someone's life.

Overcome with gratitude, despite his weakened condition, he grabbed what was left of his belongings and set off to catch her.

"Hey, Jazzi!" His voice was shaky. "Waaait uppp!"

Jazzi peered back over her shoulder but just kept walking. She had had enough drama for one day.

"Please!" Oxford shouted as he struggled to pick up his pace and ignore the stabbing pain shooting up his leg.

She stopped. "What do you want?"

"Well, I…I…" He limped closer, panting. "I want to do something to make up for what you just did for me."

"Not necessary." Jazzi tried to brush him off. "You said thanks— that's enough."

"No…no…I insist. You practically saved my life. I owe you big time!"

"Owe me? You don't owe me anything." Jazzi started to walk away. "I did what I had to do."

"C'mon, don't leave!" he pleaded.

"Really?" She turned back. "I said we're good."

"I know I don't literally *owe* you, Jazzi. It's a figure of speech," Oxford went on, "but…"

"Enough!" Jazzi was starting to get irritated with the new kid when an idea popped into her head. "Hey—are you smart? You sort of talk like you are."

The boy nodded his head vigorously and stuck out his chest. "Top honor student."

"Hmmm," she tapped her finger on her chin, "this just might work."

"Yeah?" Oxford's hopes were beginning to mount. "What might work?"

"Well, I need someone exceptionally smart to help me do my homework assignment on peace, because I have no clue what it is or where to begin. Maybe you're that someone?"

"Yes! Absolutely! I'm your man! Problem solved!" Oxford put his hand on her shoulder. "I'm on it! Consider it done! Don't give it another . . ."

"Geez, Oxy—I'm just asking you to do a homework assignment, not go on a date." Jazzi pushed his hand aside.

"Oh yeah—heh, heh." Some of the swelling had subsided, exposing a goofy grin that spread sheepishly across his face. "Guess I got carried away. When and where would you like to get started?"

"Tomorrow morning—ten-ish. What's your cell number? I'll text you when I get to the beach."

Oxford gave Jazzi his number then hobbled off toward home. The thought of meeting her the next day was a nice distraction from the unpleasant aches and pain he was feeling.

CHAPTER 2

THE OXFORD FILES

S un welcomed the first day of spring break. Jazzi sprang up in bed and pulled back the curtains. *Maybe today will be better,* she thought to herself. *Can't get much worse.* She threw on her clothes, grabbed her bold-striped beach chair, her worn-out backpack, and with her dog Nelson by her side, headed off to the beach. She loved living near the ocean—it was her favorite place to escape.

If only I could escape this stupid homework assignment, she sighed. *I mean peace . . . seriously?"* Jazzi reached over and rubbed Nelson's ears. "What was Mr. Shawnly thinking, boy? I don't know anything about peace. How could I? My parents argue over everything." She flopped back in her chair pouting and burrowed her toes into the warm California sand. "Life is so unfair."

Jazzi closed her eyes and thought about the countless nights she had lain awake in bed sobbing while her parent's battled it out in the next room. The hurt cut clear to her soul. She felt trapped inside a dark world of sadness—angry and depressed. She couldn't care less about schoolwork or poor grades. Nelson snuggled up beside her and tenderly licked her leg. He was always there for her. She looked down at him adoringly and brushed away a long corkscrew curl that had fallen down her cheek. She wasn't in the mood to fuss with her hair—she liked things simple.

Even her name was simple. Her friends had nicknamed her "Jazzi" because she loved to dance. Besides, her real name, Imo Gene Hopkins, was not something she wanted spread around school. She was sure Oxford would thank her one day for coming up with his new name—kids can be so mean.

Jazzi pulled out her sunglasses and placed them over her big blue eyes, but just as she was about to drift off into her imaginary dream world, she was startled by Nelson's bark. From out of nowhere a cloud of sand flew in all directions. A faint muffled voice grew louder and louder as someone came barreling down the beach toward them.

"Jazzi—JAZZI!" the sand-sprinter shouted. "It's me, Oxford."

There was no response.

"Whoops—I mean Oxy," he said, trying to catch his breath "Hey, I'm curious, do you have a penchant for daydreaming?"

She tipped her glasses and peeked up at their new visitor. "Mind translating that into English?"

Oxford stumbled toward her, almost tripping over her beach chair. He whipped out his tiny pocket computer and logged on. It was appropriately branded "iNo"—ready to solve any problem. He never left home without it—it was sort of his trademark. Shielding the screen with his hand, he recited, "*Penchant*: a strong desire or attraction." The bright sun flickered on his face, highlighting his wrinkled up nose and shocking red hair.

"Yeah, yeah—penchant—whatever," Jazzi muttered, rolling her eyes.

Oxford Eugene Parry, or "Oxy," as Jazzi had dubbed him, was definitely *different*. Not only was he the new kid at school, but in a very short time he had also become the target of every bully on campus. Up to this point, no one would hang out with him. Jazzi figured it was because he was, well, nerdy—but in a cool sort of way. He wore huge, too-big-for-his-face glasses and smeared tons of pink gel on his unruly red hair. Not to say he had no charm, it just showed up on rare occasions. Oxford was smart though, a real mental wizard when it came to schoolwork, plus her *penchant* for daydreaming didn't seem to bother him. Unfortunately, that was the *one* thing Jazzi's parents actually agreed on.

"Daydreaming is no excuse for poor grades," her father had told her. "If you don't shape up, you'll be spending your summer at an all-girls boarding school."

What? No boys? No freedom? NO WAAAAAAY! Jazzi knew she had to act fast, and Oxford was her only hope. So in a desperate attempt to suck up Oxford's brainpower, Jazzi appointed herself as his personalized fashion consultant—despite his protest.

"My first job will be to find you a new pair of glasses," she insisted. "Your frames are *so* yesterday!" She repositioned them on his face.

"But don't they make me look smart?"

"No, no—seriously—they don't, and what's up with the pants? They look like ancient relics you rescued from your great grandpa's Goodwill bag."

"You're joking—right?" Oxford was stunned.

Jazzi put both hands on his shoulders and looked him straight in the eyes. "Trust me, Oxy!"

"But," he confessed sadly, "I thought vintage was in."

"Vintage, yes—polyester? Borrriiing!"

"Uhh," Oxford sucked air, "so you're saying I'm not a trendsetter?"

Jazzi shook her head adamantly. She believed Oxford needed her just as much as she needed him. In her mind it was a fair exchange—his IQ for her coolness. And despite his lack of fashion sense, Jazzi was gradually growing fond of him. Beneath all the swelling and bruising, a fairly nice face had emerged. The iNo thing was annoying though.

Oxford plopped down in the sand next to her. "Okay, so when I got your text I came as fast as I could. What's the big emergency? You know we've got the whole week to finish this assignment and…"

"A *week*? A week is nothing! Don't you get it? My entire life is riding on this assignment, and if I don't ace it, my parents are sending me to an all-girls boarding school!" Her eyes welled up with tears. "Oh and did I forget to mention I'm in the middle of World War III?"

"World War—huh?" Oxford was clearly stumped.

"My parents' raging divorce battle!" She buried her face in her hands and began to weep.

"Ouch." He felt a tug at his heart. "That's painful."

"More painful than you can imagine!" Tears flowed down her cheeks. "If I flunk this peace assignment and have to go to boarding school, I'll never be able to get my family back together. I'm doomed—do you hear me? DOOMED!"

Feeling awkward, Oxford picked up a stick and threw it to Nelson. The dog looked at it lazily. Oxford kicked at the sand with his bare feet, struggling to find the right words.

"I'm sure we'll come up with something. I mean, how hard can it be to define peace?"

Jazzi grabbed her towel and wiped her eyes. "Okay, Mr. Know-It-All, tell me what it means." She threw the towel down and jumped to her feet. "C'mon, tell me. TELL ME," she hollered. "I'm waaaiiiting . . . !"

"Peace? Well, it means . . ." He stopped and pushed his glasses up higher on his nose. "It means, well, you know." He screwed up his face. "Okay, so maybe it's not that easy."

"Exactly!" Jazzi threw her hands in the air. "Defining peace when you're constantly being terrorized by bullies must get complicated."

Oxford looked away, embarrassed.

"Right, Oxy?" She poked her finger in his side. "Am I right?"

Oxford's stomach began to churn as he relived every gruesome detail of his last encounter. He wanted to forget about it, but Jazzi wouldn't back off.

"I bet having to hide in corners to keep from being tossed back and forth across campus like a hot potato, or being crammed into your locker like a wadded-up piece of paper isn't very peaceful!"

"Okay, OKAY! You've made your point, but . . ."

"But NOTHING! You may be smart but neither one of us has any peace in our life, so how in the world are we going to figure it out by next Monday?"

CHAPTER 3

A STARTLING DEVELOPMENT

O xford stood silently staring down at the ground, pondering Jazzi's question.

"Answer me, Oxford—HOW?"

"Geez, Jazzi, give me a second to recalculate our options here. You've got serious anger issues." Oxford massaged his forehead, scanning his iNo for a solution. "Okay, let me think—peace, peace…" he repeated the word over and over. "There's got to be a way—AHA!" He jumped to his feet. "I've got it!"

"What? Just like that?" Jazzi frowned with uncertainty. "You sure?"

"Yes, it's perfect. We'll call on our peers."

"Our peers? You mean the other kids in our class?" Jazzi was visibly confused. "How can they help? They've got to figure this peace thing out too."

"I'm talking kids from other countries. We're not the only ones who've ever wrestled with this issue, you know." Oxford was clearly getting worked up. "Everyone's looking for peace—it's a universal quest."

Jazzi thought a minute. "Okay, so let me get this straight. By contacting these other kids…"

Oxford cut her off excitedly. "We find out how *they* would define peace. This is huge, Jazzi!" His eyes gleamed. "Just imagine, if we combine our universal brainpower, this assignment will be a piece of cake."

Jazzi listened closely as Oxford continued to plead his case, hoping to muster up some enthusiasm. "So you're saying that through some super-social-conversational highway connecting us to our international peers, we're going to find our answer?"

"Exactly!" Oxford glowed with excitement.

"Well, good luck with that," she said, throwing her arms up. "I need more convincing."

Oxford smiled. "Have a little faith, Jazzi, I believe the answer's right in front of your face." He nodded toward his backpack where he had his notepad safely secured.

"Your notepad?" She blew a curl out of her eye.

"Yes, we'll create a website and call it—I don't know—maybe 'Kids' Worldwide Peace Club'? Something like that."

"Hmmm…," Jazzi wondered aloud, "not sure where that came from, but I sort of like it."

"Finally," Oxford said, beaming. "You with me now? It will be our own generation's opinions. We'll pick the brains of kids from different cultures and backgrounds from all around the world and *voila*!"

Jazzi watched on eagerly as Oxford's brain went into overdrive, and it was at that point she knew she had made the right choice. If she could complete her peace assignment with a passing grade and make her parents happy—she was sure she could get them back together. That would make Oxford, not only her hero, but her new BFF. It was meant to be! Her mind continued to wander as she gazed out across the water, imagining all the kids on the other side of the Pacific Ocean. *Do you have the answers we're looking for? Do you know what peace is?*

Mesmerized by the sun's glistening rays dancing gracefully over the bewitching blue sea, Jazzi was quickly swept back into reality when the crack and boom of smashing surf beckoned.

"WOO-HOO!" she shouted at the top of her lungs. "GO FOR IT, GENIUS!" She pulled her T-shirt over her head and stripped down to her swimsuit. "Check outside—those waves are huge! I'm on it!" She waved to Oxford and took off running.

Oxford shook his head grinning and began to type away. He figured Jazzi couldn't resist the call of the ocean and there was nothing he could say or do to keep her focused. This project was now in his lap.

Nelson's eyes followed Jazzi as she dashed toward the surf, leaving only a trail of footprints in the sand. The fresh scent of saltwater mixed with a hint of seaweed filled her senses as she leapt headlong into the first peaking wave, completely unaware of the enormous swell forming behind it. She popped her head up to catch her breath but before she had a chance, an avalanche of water came crashing down on her, twisting her around and around like the spin cycle of a washing machine. She struggled to free herself, but each time another wave pounded her back down to the ocean floor. Over and under, the waves continued to twirl her about, forcing her to swallow massive amounts of saltwater. She gasped desperately for air.

Nelson, sensing danger, started running around in circles, barking as loud as he could. He was trying to alert Oxford to the impending catastrophe, but Oxford was too caught up in their homework assignment to notice. Finally Nelson pounced up on his lap and began howling.

"Stop it, Nelson!" Oxford pushed him off. "What are you doing?"

But Nelson wasn't about to stop. He continued to jump up again and again until finally Oxford had no choice but to look up. He was just in time to see the riptide rushing back to sea, leaving Jazzi's motionless body half-buried in the wet sand. With a bursting upspring, Oxford dropped his notepad and rushed down to see what was wrong. By the time he reached Jazzi, she was sprawled out on the beach like a ragdoll—barely breathing. Quickly Oxford put his lifeguard skills to work and began to administer CPR. Nelson crouched close by Jazzi's side, nudging her lovingly with his paw.

"One-two-three-BREATHE! One-two-three…," Oxford cried out to Jazzi with every push. "BREATHE, Jazzi . . . two-three…!" Unexpectedly her body heaved and saltwater gushed from her mouth, completely drenching him. He let out a high-pitched squeal and continued on. "Jazzi—JAZZI, can you hear me?" He put his head on her chest to see if she was breathing. Nelson nuzzled his cold clammy nose into her side whimpering, but other than an occasional gasp for air, she remained still.

Oxford looked down, discouraged. "C'mon, Jazzi…" he pleaded, "please don't give up. Look at me!"

But before he could utter another word, both of her eyelids popped open like some zombie creature in a horror flick. He stood there powerless, staring down into a pair of dark, distant, unfamiliar eyes.

"Jazzi?" He waved his hand back and forth across her face, "You in there? Hellooooo…?"

In her trancelike state, Jazzi is mysteriously taken aback by a vibrant pop of color that illuminates all around her. Like magic she floats outside her body into a realm beyond her own— the world takes on new dimension. Everything is much more alive than before. She stares blankly up at Oxford, her mind racing with bizarre images. Still she remains silent, unsure of what is real and what is imaginary.

Oxford fought to hold back the tears, fearing the worst, and then he heard a small voice whisper, "Where am I?"

"Jazzi?" Oxford let out an agonizing sigh of relief. "You're alive? Oh, thank God!" He gently stroked her cheek. "You're ALIVE!"

Nelson ran around in circles, shivering with excitement.

Jazzi rubbed her eyes confused as her body lay trembling in the wet sand. "What's that awful noise? Why is everything shaking?" She grimaced. "Make it stop!"

"Noise? Shaking?" Oxford looked around, baffled. "What are you talking about?"

"Listen!" Jazzi groaned and poked her fingers in her ears, trying to silence the deafening roar.

"WHOA!" Oxford hollered when a spiraling funnel of wind and sand appeared from out of nowhere and instantly swept the three friends off their feet. Instinctively, Oxford stretched out his arm and scooped up their backpacks. In the blink of an eye, they were airborne and spinning utterly out of control.

"You mean *that* noise?" Oxford wrenched as a sudden burst of wind pushed him higher, causing him to feel woozy.

"YES . . . WHAT'S HAP . . . PEN . . . NING . . . OXEEEEEE . . . ?" Jazzi screeched.

"MY GUESS IS WE'RE ROTATING INSIDE A VIOLENT COLUMN OF AIR!"

"AIR?" Jazzi spun around in circles, her hair flying every which way. "WHAT?" Nelson somersaulted beside her, wagging his tail trustingly.

"Tornado, Jazzi—WE'RE TRAPPED INSIDE A TORNADO!"

"But that's IMPOSSIBLE! How will we get down?"

"YIKES!" Oxford wailed as a surge of wind propelled him into an upside down plié. "COULD BE A PROBLEM . . . !"

Before Oxford could complete his sentence, the raging funnel began to lose momentum, and the loss of force sent the three pals spiraling downward straight toward the beach.

"BRACE YOURSELF, JAZZI. THIS WON'T BE PLEASANT!"

Jazzi closed her eyes as she hit the sand with a hard thump. "OUCH!" She groaned and rubbed her thigh.

Nelson was second in line, howling nervously all the way down. He bounced across the sand like a wayward Frisbee and landed topsy-turvy on his back next to Jazzi. A few seconds later a series of piercing cries prompted Jazzi and Nelson to look up just in time to see Oxford doing a face plant into a nearby pile of sand—backpacks still secured to his arm.

"Wow, I'm blown away!" he said, spitting out a mouthful of sand. "Get it, Jazzi? Tornado—blown away?" Oxford was trying his best to make Jazzi laugh despite their stressful situation, but she wasn't buying it.

"Okay, I get it, Oxy, I GET IT! Just tell me why everything looks so… so…?"

"Different?" Oxford made a painful expression as he completed her sentence.

"Yes!" She glanced around. "Different. I mean, I know we're in San Diego, but somethings not right—it feels weird. I don't know if I'm dreaming or losing my mind?"

"Is that a multiple-choice question?" Oxford gave a slight grin.

"This is not the time to make jokes. I'm serious." Jazzi buried her face between her knees and signaled Nelson to cuddle up beside her. "Some nightmare, huh, boy?"

"Believe me, Jazzi, I wish I knew, because…" Oxford looked from side to side, scratching his head, "whatever is happening to you—is happening to me."

"But you're the one with all the answers." Jazzi flopped back on her elbows and sighed. "Please say you have it under control." She looked at him with hopeless eyes.

Oxford scooted up next to her. "We're going to be fine, Jazzi. Don't worry."

"You mean it, Oxy?"

CHAPTER 4

LOOKING FOR PEACE IN ALL THE WRONG PLACES

Jazzi peered down at the ground, discouraged, when a small red crab shimmied sideways up alongside her. "Hey," she curled up her toes, "you startled me."

The crab stopped and looked her up and down as if he were studying her, then blurted out as plain as day, "You aware of today's headlines, Miss?"

Jazzi's mouth dropped open. "What?" She leaned over to get a closer look. "You can talk?"

A look of disgust spread across the crab's face. "You're talking to me, aren't you?"

She turned to Oxford. "Crabby little guy."

"Well of course I'm crabby! No peace in the Middle East and CrabRon Energy Stocks plummet? Why wouldn't I be?" He read

20

from a tiny device clenched between his claws. "What's this world coming to?"

Jazzi put her hands to her face. "Okay, now I know I'm dreaming!" She and Oxford watched stunned as the peculiar little creature scurried off across her feet. It was if he had some important business to tend to.

Oxford jumped up. "C'mon, let's follow him." He grabbed Jazzi's arm and jerked her to her feet.

"Not so fast there, buddy." She swayed back and forth trying to get her balance.

"Sorry," Oxford said with a sense of urgency, "but we can't let that crab get away."

"What?" Jazzi frowned. "Guess I am a little hungry—crab sounds good."

Nelson's ears perked up when he heard the word *crab*. He was poised and ready to pounce on the snappy little crustacean first chance he got.

"Hey, hey, hey . . ." Oxford shook his head, disgusted. "I'm not talking crab cocktail here."

Jazzi scrunched her forehead.

"Look, we have to do something, Jazzi. We can't sit here all day and speculate." Oxford was clearly frustrated.

Dumbfounded by their strange new environment, Oxford was desperate for answers and willing to try anything. Following a crab was a stretch but—why not? Nothing had made sense so far. Together they brushed themselves off, gathered up their gear, and set out eagerly to catch up to the sandy little critter.

The trio followed the crab as it scuttled around a bend and into a hidden cove. Once it realized it was being followed, it sped off and vanished between two rocks.

"Well, that was a waste of time," Oxford grunted.

"Maybe not," said Jazzi, "Look—over there!" She pointed at something strange near the far end of the cove. "Is *that* what I think it is?"

"I hope not," said Oxford, cleaning his glasses to get a better look, "but what do you think it is?"

"A pirate ship? Yeah, I think it's a pirate ship." Jazzi grabbed Oxford's arm. "Let's go find out!"

"S-S-S-Sure." Oxford walked reluctantly, nervously wringing his sweaty hands.

As they got closer it became apparent Jazzi was right, much to Oxford's demise. Partially washed up on the shoreline, covered with green slimy moss and tangled-up seaweed, an old shipwrecked schooner sat teetering on a mound of sand. Above it a torn sail, complete with skull and crossbones, rippled in the misty afternoon breeze. On the ship's deck, watching Jazzi's and Oxford's every move, stood a dark menacing pirate. The midday sun cast distorted shadows over the frightening figure.

Jazzi and Oxford stared uneasily as he stepped into their view—his piercing blue eyes shot back like darts at the daring young intruders. He was decked out in full pirate regalia, yet filthy and unkempt. A shiny sword swayed hypnotically back and forth at his side, while flocks of birds circled relentlessly overhead.

Jazzi mustered up some courage and started walking toward the pirate. Oxford grabbed her arm. "Are you crazy? He could be dangerous!"

"Look, Oxy, I was practically swallowed up by the sea, engulfed inside a giant spinning sand cone, dropped onto some mysterious beach, and just finished chasing a talking crab for some unknown reason."

"Yeah—so?"

"So what makes you think I can't handle some weirdo wannabe pirate? Besides," her tone softened, "he may have the answer we're looking for."

Oxford gulped. "Or not."

"What—ya gonna let a little fear get in the way?"

"Maybe."

Jazzi shook Oxford's hand off impatiently and continued to walk on. Nelson trailed close behind.

"I'm not so sure about this, Jazzi." Oxford hesitated a moment then quickly ran to catch up. "Don't say I didn't warn you!"

"Ahoy, mate!" Jazzi called up to the pirate as they neared the shipwrecked schooner.

He had alluring blue eyes that narrowed as he squinted in the bright midday sun. "What are ya lookin' fer—buried treasure?" He chuckled—the glare from his flashy gold tooth nearly blinded them.

"Actually, we're looking for," Jazzi paused, making direct eye contact with the filthy old pirate, "peace!"

"Peace, eh? How's that working fer ya?"

"Not so good," she replied. Oxford and Nelson stood close by looking up at the pirate, not making a peep.

"Well it be yer lucky day then, lass. Ye be looking at the world's only peaceful pirate." He grinned down at them with an upturned lip, rolling his mustache between two fingers.

Oxford cleared his throat timidly. "I've never heard of a peaceful pirate. Isn't fighting part of your job description?"

"ARRRRRRGH," he snarled.

"Excuse me?" Jazzi crossed her arms and frowned.

"Whot? Ye never heard pirate talk before?"

"And just what exactly does 'arrrrrgh' mean?" She stood defiant.

"Why everyone knows its pirate lingo fer shalom."

"Shalom?" Jazzi looked at Oxford.

Oxford adjusted his glasses and stepped forward with his iNo. "I believe shalom means peace in Hebrew. It's also a greeting for hello and goodbye, so I highly doubt arrrrrgh and shalom are synonymous."

"Now, now, don't ye be too quick to judge." He waved his finger back and forth in a scolding like manner.

Jazzi gazed up at the pirate with her hands on her hips. "Well, saying 'arrrrrgh' doesn't exactly make you a peace expert."

"No?" He leaned over the side of the schooner, swinging his sword inches from their throats.

"See!" Jazzi jumped back. "You call that peaceful?"

Oxford elbowed Jazzi nervously. "It's getting ugly!"

"I'll show ye peace," the pirate muttered. "C'mere, young lass. I'll tell ye a li'l secret." He beckoned her with a crooked finger.

Oxford cried out. "Don't listen to him, Jazzi!"

But it was too late. Quick as a wink the pirate reached down, grabbed Jazzi by both arms, and hauled her up over the side. She kicked and screamed with all her might, but it was no use. The ornery old pirate picked up a burlap bag, threw it over her head then dragged her to the end of a long wooden plank.

Oxford paced nervously back and forth, feeling helpless as he watched Jazzi dangling over the treacherous water but—what could he do?

CHAPTER 5

STUCK IN THE MUCK

"L ET THE SHOW BEGIN!" The pirate swung out his arm, shouting gleefully as if he were introducing a premier Hollywood production.

Instantly, man-eating sharks began circling below—ravenous jaws snapped anxiously for their next juicy meal.

"Help me!" Jazzi's muffled voice pleaded from inside the bag. "Get me out of here!"

Nelson raced back and forth, unleashing a series of deep guttural snarls and growls, all the while Jazzi continued to kick and scream.

Finally, Oxford had had enough. With a rush of adrenaline surging through his body, he barreled up to the side of the ship and started climbing. "I DEMAND YOU RELEASE HER THIS INSTANT!" he shrieked.

Then, lo and behold, that's just what the shady old pirate did. Oxford, shocked at the sudden turn of events, lost his grip and fell flat on his butt. "OW!" He discreetly rubbed his derriere.

"I said get me outta here!" Jazzi demanded again.

"Hang on, lass, I'm doing my best. There's a gall durn knot in the rope." The pirate pulled out his sword and began to tug away at the knot, cursing the whole time under his breath. Oxford watched confused as the pirate struggled to untie the ropes and pull the bag off Jazzi's head. She stood there stunned, wobbling back and forth, trying to catch her breath.

"But…but…," Oxford stammered, shaking his head. "I thought…"

"I know, I know, you thought I was really going to drop her. I was testing you, my good man."

"Why would you do such a mean thing?" Oxford picked himself up, shouting back the question.

"Shhhhh…," The pirate held his finger to his lips. "Relax, mate." His speech became more refined. "You lacked courage, young man. I gave you the chance to be bold and brave so you could rescue your fair young maiden." The pirate let out a big belly laugh. "You know I could never actually kill someone, but my cousin Vinny—well…" he chuckled, "every family's got one." He broke into a big toothy grin—his gold tooth gleaming.

Jazzi stood with her hands on her hips glaring at him. "You should be ashamed of yourself!" She peered over the side of the boat at the hungry sharks below. "I could have been catch of the day!"

"Oh, those?" He held up a remote control. "Impressive, eh? They're robots."

"WHAT?" Jazzi barked.

Oxford stood speechless, stunned by this so-called prank.

"Relax, relax, I'm just playing the part of the villain, immersing myself in my role like any method actor would." He winked. "But enough about me—you two are on a quest."

Oxford looked at him suspiciously. "How did you know that?"

He laughed. "Come inside. There's something I want to show you."

Before Oxford could protest, Jazzi pushed him through the doorway. "It's okay, Oxy. He didn't kill me."

"Yet," he muttered to himself.

One by one they stepped carefully into the musky wooden cabin. Several noisy birds squawked and took flight, repositioning themselves into other parts of the room. The walls were dark mahogany and smelled of mold. Torn scarlet velvet drapes with shredded gold tassels hung unevenly over the windows. In the center of the room sat a partially opened treasure chest, which immediately caught Nelson's attention. He stuck his nose deep inside and began sniffing around. Before long his head popped up holding a packet of birdseed wedged between his teeth.

Oxford walked over to get a closer look. "Birdseed? You have birdseed inside your treasure chest?" he asked, puzzled. "That's weird."

"Why would you say that?"

"I don't know, guess I always imagined a treasure chest being filled with real treasure, like gold and silver coins."

"Everyone's treasure is different. To a hungry bird this is the greatest treasure there is." The pirate spoke like a protective father.

"Okay, that makes sense," Oxford agreed.

"Nelson, put the treasure back, boy!" Jazzi scolded him.

Nelson quickly obeyed and dropped the seeds back into the chest. It did seem odd to find a treasure chest filled with birdseed though. Jazzi turned toward the pirate and apologized for Nelson's behavior. He simply nodded and began to speak.

"My name is Sir Sean, and I am the keeper of these jabbering birds." He removed his hat and bowed. "And you," he pointed to them one at a time, "are Jazzi and Oxford."

Their mouths dropped open in astonishment.

"Oh, and I can't leave out Nelson," he added.

"But how do you know who we are?" asked Jazzi.

"Yeah," said Oxford. "How?"

"Well," he smiled devilishly, "it may surprise you to learn that I know more about the three of you than you know about yourselves."

Oxford shifted uncomfortably from one foot to the other.

Sir Sean twirled the ends of his mustache. "Curious, are we?"

Jazzi nodded her head vigorously.

"You're also puzzled about your whereabouts and where to go from here."

Oxford squirmed as he turned to face Jazzi. "We are kind of stuck."

"Stuck, eh? Perhaps this will help." Sir Sean pulled an old coffee-stained map from his coat pocket. The three adventurers eagerly crowded closer.

"A treasure map?" Oxford asked, enchanted. "Wait—will it lead us to birdseed?"

The pirate let out a belly laugh. "Sorry to disappoint you, lad, but this map will prove to be much more valuable." He pressed the map out flat on the table, marked it with a red X, scribbled something on the back, and then carefully handed it to Jazzi.

"What's the red X for?" asked Oxford.

"It's the key to your entire quest. You must go exactly where it takes you."

Jazzi and Oxford were all ears while Nelson sat by obediently.

"Don't be frightened when the X moves or you see things out of the ordinary. It's all part of the journey." The pirate turned to walk away and then suddenly stopped. "Be forewarned," he said with a stern voice as he peered back over one shoulder. "No matter what happens—DO NOT lose the map! Now be off with ye. I've got feathered friends to tend to." He beamed mischievously while humming a catchy little pirate ditty under his breath.

"Gosh." Jazzi hugged the map. "This is serious. I'd better guard it with my life."

"He was pretty clear, Jazzi." Oxford tapped his finger on his chin. "We lose *it*—we lose *everything!*"

The kids had a lot on their minds as they said goodbye to the pirate and exited the ship. Heading off on an unknown adventure was both exciting and scary. It was that *unknown* part that had them concerned. They had barely made it to the bottom of the ramp when something caught Oxford's attention. He stopped dead in his tracks, unable to speak. Nelson's fur bristled as he sat back on all fours, not uttering a peep. But Jazzi? Well, she was too busy removing bird feathers from her hair to notice anything.

"Look!" Oxford pointed up in the direction of the ship. Jazzi slowly turned around—her jaw instantly fell open. But before she could say anything, they heard Sir Sean's voice shouting in the distance, "ONCE YOU BEGIN YOUR QUEST—*NEVER* GIVE UPPPPP...!"

His voice soon faded away and then—POOF! Right before their eyes Sir Sean and his entire ship completely disappeared—as if it had never existed. The two friends looked at each other in disbelief. They stared at the space where the schooner had just been, uncertain of what had just happened. Oxford rubbed his eyes and slowly turned toward Jazzi. Together they looked down at the map in Jazzi's hand.

"Can we trust the word of a pirate who just vanished into thin air?" Oxford asked, worried.

Jazzi shrugged. "Strangely, I believe him."

CHAPTER 6
SU AND
CAT-MAN-DOO

C'mon," Oxford urged, motioning to Jazzi and Nelson, "let's get out of here."

Nelson led the way as the two friends raced frantically down the beach, arm in arm. Suddenly Jazzi stopped.

"What's wrong?" Oxford panted. "The vanishing ship thing creep you out?"

"Sorta, but—umm—think it's more about what he yelled as he was fading out of sight."

"Okay—go on." Oxford encouraged her.

"Well, he said, 'Once you begin your quest, never give up'."

"Yes, I heard that." Oxford nodded.

"So does that mean we're going to *want* to give up? I mean, what does he know that we don't?"

"That's what we're going to find out. There are many missing pieces to this puzzle," Oxford insisted. "Does the map show we're getting close to anything?"

"Yes, I think so." She opened it up. "According to the red X, we're close to...,"

"Listen!" Oxford interrupted. "What's that noise?"

"Not another noise." Jazzi cringed.

Nelson started to growl as an unfamiliar whistling echoed down the beach and strangely surrounded them. Jazzi and Oxford stood very still trying to figure out where it was coming from.

Oxford knelt down and pressed his ear to the ground. "It seems to be coming from underneath the sand."

Nelson immediately raced over to Oxford's side and began digging frantically. A high rooster-tail of sand flew between his hind legs. Then, just as quickly as he started, he stopped and slowly backed away as the hole began to grow larger and larger all by itself. The last little bit of sand slid down into the opening, and then, lo and behold, a boy climbed out.

"No way!" Oxford stepped back and fumbled for his iNo.

Jazzi stood paralyzed. She couldn't take her eyes off the sand-covered boy that just appeared from out of nowhere. He looked about their age, eleven or twelve, and he appeared to be Asian. He wore the most eye-catching hot pink and yellow sneakers, along with skinny black jeans and a white T-shirt that read, "I luv 0101110." He had a cell phone clutched in his right hand, and strapped to his left arm was an elastic cord that stretched back down inside the hole.

"Who-are-you?" Jazzi was careful to pronounce each word very slowly. "And-what-planet-did-you-come-from?"

The boy flashed a big smile—his pearly white teeth sparkled against his caramel-colored skin. A fringe of shiny dark bangs framed his face.

"My name is Su," he said with a faint accent.

"A boy named Sue?" Jazzi giggled. "That's a girl's name."

"Not Sue. It's Su, Su Sing Yu. I'm from China," the boy said proudly.

"That's impossible," Oxford sputtered. "China is on the other side of the world."

"That is correct," he nodded.

Jazzi and Oxford continued to check out their new arrival, intrigued by the mysterious elastic cord that was attached to his wrist. Oxford was just about to quiz him about it when Su suddenly lifted his arm. The cord sprang forth like a rocket, flinging a multicolored, flat-faced, fur-ball upside down on Nelson's head. A long white-tipped tail whipped back and forth in front of Nelson's eyes. Without warning, the creature bared its claws, sinking them deep into Nelson's sensitive nose.

"YEOWWW!" Nelson howled.

"Mew," purred the fur-ball.

Oxford turned to Jazzi, "Mystery solved."

"Is that a CAT BURIED in my DOG'S FACE?" Jazzi shrieked.

Su nodded cheerfully. "That's my feisty feline friend, Cat-Man-Doo. Seems to like your dog. By the way, where am I and who are you?"

"Nice…," Jazzi muttered to herself, irritated. She walked over and carefully peeled the furry creature off of Nelson's head.

"Why was your cat strapped to your wrist?" Oxford asked.

"Didn't want her to get lost," answered Su.

"Oh yeah, I can see how that might be a concern," Oxford said sarcastically. "It's not like China is right around the corner."

Su smiled back. "Exactly."

Oxford shook his head, surprised by Su's remark, then proceeded with introductions. "My name is Oxford and this . . . ta daaa . . ." he bowed and held out his arm, "is Jazzi!"

Jazzi gave Su a slight nod. "And this is my dog Nelson who, by the way, is feeling much better now that I've removed that fur-ball from his cranium." Nelson wagged his tail in agreement.

"Getting back to your question," Oxford continued, "you're in San Diego, California, which is in the United States, of course. Now my question is, how did you allegedly get here all the way from China?"

"It's a long story," said Su.

"We've got time." Oxford folded his arms.

"Or do we?" Jazzi frowned, impatiently tapping her foot.

"Well," Oxford corrected himself, "a little time."

Jazzi rolled her eyes, slightly agitated. "Please tell us how you got here, Su," she said, holding up the map Sir Sean had given her, "and why this map just *happens* to have a big red X on the exact spot where you just popped up. I don't get it."

There appeared to be a lot of holes in their new companion's story, and Jazzi and Oxford were going to get to the bottom of it.

CHAPTER 7

CYBER-*WHAT!*

W e need to chat, Su," said Jazzi. "Follow me."

Su and Cat-Man-Doo followed Jazzi, Oxford, and Nelson down the beach to the end of a long boardwalk. They pushed their gear to the side and sat on the edge of the pier, dangling their legs over the dark blue-green water.

"So, Su," Jazzi said, swinging her feet impatiently, "what's with the hole in the sand? You don't actually expect us to believe you climbed all the way here from China?"

"Of course not. I rode the CyberCoaster through countless numbers of underground tunnels."

"Underground tunnels? Cyber-*what*?!" Oxford broke into a cold sweat as he frantically scrolled through his iNo.

"It's called a CyberCoaster," Su corrected him, "not Cyber-what."

"Yeah—that!" said Oxford, perspiring. "Never heard of such a thing, and underground tunnels?" He held up his trusty device. "When I do a word search it says it cannot be found."

"Hmmm," Su rubbed his chin, "not surprising. It surpasses mere human logic. The CyberCoaster is like nothing you could ever imagine. It hovers above an underground track that circles the entire earth and comes complete with a personalized cyberite. It's been around forever."

"That's insane!" Oxford replied. "What's a cyberite?"

"Umm, I believe the best way to describe a cyberite would be to call it a non-gender, high-tech flight attendant that knows your needs and desires before you do." Su grinned.

"Like a robot?" asked Jazzi.

Su nodded. "With the exception that it has feelings and emotions."

"That's unbelievable!" Jazzi gushed.

"Yeah, a little *too* unbelievable if you ask me," echoed Oxford. "So, really, Su, why are you here? You didn't just drop by for pizza."

"Good question. I downloaded 'peace' thinking it would take me to New York City, you know, home of the Big Apple? Somehow I miscalculated."

"I'm confused." Jazzi scrunched her forehead. "Why New York? Why peace?"

"It's simple. I am doing research for a homework assignment on peace and…"

"Dude!" Oxford interrupted. "You so desperate for an A that you would travel clear across the continent on some contraption that…"

"CyberCoaster is the word I believe you're looking for." Su nodded politely.

"Wait—WHAT?" Jazzi held her hand up to silence Oxford. "Did you just say *peace* assignment?"

"Yes, can you believe that?" Su laughed. "Maybe it's just me, but *peace*—really? Open your eyes and look around—hardly a peaceful world."

Jazzi's eyes lit up. "Go on, Su, don't leave me hanging. This is all starting to make sense now."

"Alright," he smiled, "if you insist."

"I absolutely do!" she beamed.

"I knew it was a long shot, but I had read somewhere that the United Nations was called a 'House of Peace'. I thought maybe if I went there in person I could get what I needed to complete my ridiculous assignment. I mapped out a course and planned on making this a one-stop shop, but for whatever reason I landed in San Diego."

Jazzi squealed, "This is no accident, Su, its fate! I bet we're supposed to go to New York with you." She quickly searched for New York on the map. "Right, Oxy?"

"Uh, sure, I guess," Oxford replied halfheartedly. "Is there an X over New York?"

"Well, no, but so what? Who says it won't move?" Jazzi winked. "Remember Sir Sean said to expect change."

Su held out his hand. "May I review the map please?" He studied it carefully. "That's odd, you don't have a final destination."

Jazzi and Oxford looked at each other and then turned back to Su.

"Well, that's not exactly true," Jazzi replied vaguely. "We're just not sure where it is at this particular moment."

"What Jazzi means," Oxford joined in, "is that our instructions were very explicit— follow the red X—period.

"Yeah," Jazzi nodded, "and as long as we complete our assignment do we really care where we end up? It'll be kind of a mystery tour."

"Trust me," Su smiled, "this will be an experience you'll never forget!"

Jazzi grabbed Su's arm and pulled him to his feet. "I believe you! C'mon, what are we waiting for? You've got to show us that cyber-thingy and the underground tunnels—how they work, where they go, and... "

"WHOA, whoa, whoaaaa…!" Oxford gave Jazzi a slight punch on her shoulder. "Just curious, are you planning on letting your parents in on this little adventure?"

There was no reply.

Oxford turned and looked Jazzi straight in the eyes then leaned in as close as he could so Su couldn't hear. "You honestly think we should just leave and not tell anyone?" He whispered fiercely in her ear. "Because I'm pretty certain that this gnawing sensation in my gut is a telltale sign that it's not a good idea."

Jazzi remained silent.

"Did you hear me, Jazzi?" Oxford grabbed her arm and pulled her toward him—he could see the anger in her eyes.

CHAPTER 8

LIVING ON THE EDGE

L et go of me, Oxford!" Jazzi trembled as she shoved his hand away. "I heard you the first time but, guess what? I can't worry about my parents right now, okay? Tomorrow's another day." She looked away bitterly. "Besides they don't care about me." She fought back a tear. "If they did, they wouldn't be getting divorced!"

"Excuse us, Su, we need a minute to discuss a private matter," Oxford apologized.

Su got up and walked over to Nelson and Cat-Man-Doo—they seemed to be getting along fine.

"Quit being so stubborn, Jazzi. Their divorce has nothing to do with you. They're caught up in their own stuff right now, so quit blaming yourself." Oxford tried desperately to convince her.

"Stop it, Oxy, I said it didn't matter. I don't *need* their approval, and I'm certainly not looking for yours."

"Okay, okay—sorry. Just hate to see you go through more grief, that's all." He knew it was time to drop the subject.

Jazzi took a deep breath and stuffed back her anger. "I'll deal with it *my* way, thank you."

Oxford pulled out his iNo and sent his parents a text message letting them know he was with Jazzi and not to worry.

"Put that thing down!" Jazzi huffed then turned to Su. In her sweetest voice she cooed, "We're ready to go, Su."

Su walked up to Oxford. "You up for this?"

"Sure," Oxford nodded begrudgingly. "It's Jazzi's way or no way."

"Exactly," she agreed. "Now if you'll just trust Su, everything will be fine."

Oxford bit his tongue to avoid any further comments—there was no way he was going to trust some kid who had just climbed out of a hole in the sand.

Together with Nelson and Cat-Man-Doo, Jazzi and Oxford tagged behind Su until they reached the spot on the beach where he had first appeared.

"WOO-HOO!" Jazzi waved the map around. "It's like finding buried treasure!"

Su quickly went to work brushing away the sand. Eventually, it caved in on its own, exposing the hole he had recently climbed out of. He attached the elastic strap to Cat-Man-Doo and began to climb in. "Stay close to me," he warned. "It's a maze down there, and you'd never find your way back on your own. It can also get slippery, so watch your step."

Despite Oxford's apprehension, he agreed to follow. "Does Nelson need a leash?" he asked Jazzi.

"No, he's fine," Jazzi assured him. "He rarely leaves my side."

Su led the way with his flashlight while Jazzi and Oxford stayed close behind as instructed. Around and around they went, slowly descending down a long winding staircase into the alluring hole.

"This is creepy, Su!" Jazzi cringed. "I can hardly see." She blinked her eyes several times trying to focus. "Plus I'm starting to feel claustrophobic."

Her voice echoed through the tunnel as they spiraled deeper and deeper into inky blackness. "Isn't there another way down?"

"Yes," Oxford concurred, "an alternate route would be nice."

"Trust me," Su said reassuringly, "you're fine, but watch your step."

"Trust?" Oxford shuddered. "There's that word again."

Jazzi and Oxford continued to trail Su. The farther they descended the damper and more slippery it became. The musky smell of mold permeated the air and, to make matters worse, Su's flashlight kept flickering on and off. Just as Jazzi was about to take another step down, her heel slipped off the edge causing her to lose her balance and plummet headfirst over the side of the staircase.

"AAAHHH," she wailed as she went tumbling over the rail. Nelson barked frantically as he watched her struggling to grab Oxford's hand.

"SAVE MEEEEEE . . . !" she screamed.

Oxford immediately stretched out both arms to grab her, but her hand slipped right through his sweaty palms. Waves of adrenaline surged through his veins as he stretched over the rail as far as he could in a desperate attempt to snag her shirtsleeve.

"Su!" Oxford yelled. "I need your help!" It took every ounce of muscle he had to hold on. "Hurry—her sleeve is starting to rip!"

"OHHH, I can't look!" Jazzi's body trembled with fear as she hung defenseless over a pit of unknown entities.

Su rushed back up the stairs to assist Oxford. He leaned over the rail and snatched the back of Jazzi's shirt. Together they slowly pulled her up, inch by inch. Oxford could hardly see. The sweat from his forehead was fogging up his glasses. The more he strained, the more he sweated—the more he sweated, the foggier they became. Then, just when it seemed completely hopeless, both boys mustered up every bit of strength they had and with one final yank, pulled Jazzi back up over the rail to safety.

"That was close, Jazzi," Su scolded. "Pay more attention to where you step."

Oxford agreed. Still panting, he sat down on the step so he could clean his glasses. Suddenly his face went white. "Jazzi— the map? OH NO—did you drop the MAP?"

Jazzi gave a hint of a smile as she lay quietly on the cold staircase trying to catch her breath. Her stretched out T-shirt now looked like an oversized poncho as she raised her arm and slowly waved the map.

"Oh, thank you, thank you," he said, grabbing his chest. "We CAN'T lose it!"

"I know, Oxy, I know." She took a deep breath and stroked her leg. "But can I just have a moment to regroup?"

"Of course, what was I thinking?"

"C'mon you two. Don't wimp out on me now. We're almost at the bottom." Su pointed his flashlight down the staircase.

Oxford held out his hand. "Can you make it, Jazzi?"

She looked at her dirty hands, then wiped them on her jeans. "Yup, I'm fine."

"We've got an assignment to complete, people," Su yelled impatiently. "Granted it's a stupid assignment, but you with me or not?"

"You really think searching for peace is stupid?" Jazzi asked.

"Not if you believe it's real." Su showed no emotion. "I just haven't seen it. You know in my country the government only allows one kid per family. Imagine the pressure I'm under being the only son. I have no choice but to succeed—hardly peaceful. Kids in the USA have it easy if you ask me."

Jazzi pondered Su's remark as she continued to rub her sore leg. She didn't fully understand Su's culture, but she hoped he was wrong about peace. What if he wasn't? What if this whole peace journey proved to be a hoax? There was only a small window of time before the assignment was due, and Oxford was right, her parents would go ballistic once they discovered she was missing.

Pressure was mounting, but the anticipation of what Jazzi was hoping to experience at the bottom of the cave overshadowed her frightful ordeal.

Cat-Man-Doo pranced ahead of Su, stretching the elastic band to its limit, while Nelson remained close to Jazzi. They finally reached the bottom and stepped out onto a sturdy wooden platform.

Jazzi stood gazing about, she was at a loss for words. "Am I dreaming?" She was completely awestruck by their new environment. She ran her fingers across one of the cave walls where famous names had been carved in the stone.

Oxford stared speechless.

"Over here," Su called and shone his flashlight across other walls. "Check it out."

Jazzi began reading names out loud: "Walt Disney, Marilyn Monroe, Ronald Reagan, Julia Child…," The list went on and on.

"Why are all these names on the wall, Su?" Oxford was intrigued. "Have these people actually been here?"

Su nodded. "These tunnels have been around for some time, but only those who are enlightened can travel through them."

"What do you mean, enlightened?" asked Jazzi.

"I mean it takes the gift of imagination to see beyond the natural. Not everyone has it."

"We must be special then." Jazzi curtsied as if she were on stage.

"We'll see just *how* special," Oxford grunted.

Jazzi and Oxford were awestruck when an all-encompassing luminescence began to surround them. Su turned off his flashlight for a better visual effect. Everywhere they turned there were bright lights bouncing like laser beams off of jewel-colored shards of rock. They jutted up majestically from the ground and cascaded down from the ceiling. It was spectacular!

"Check out the bling on those oversized monster fangs," Jazzi squealed.

Oxford grabbed his iNo, preparing to educate. "Actually those are called stalactites, Jazzi, and the ones jutting up from the ground are called stalagmites. They are deposits, usually made of calcium carbonate. Notice they're shaped like icicles."

"Whatever you say, Oxy. I bet there's enough voltage down here to light up an entire shopping mall."

On the wall across from the platform was a sign that read "You Are Here."

"So, Su," quizzed Oxford, "how does your CyberCoaster move?"

"It's transported by vibrations of energy combined with the force of gravity. Magnets on the external frame are connected to a steering device in the control mechanism, and they shift and slide to determine the direction."

Jazzi listened dumbfounded—technology didn't interest her.

"Simply stated, I guess you could say it's pushed and pulled wherever it goes, yet the direction is entirely up to us."

"But we are going to follow the map, right, Su?" Jazzi asked, concerned.

"Your wish is my command, Jazzi." Su bowed. "We shall follow the path of the mysterious red X to the bitter end."

"I'm good with that," she giggled.

Oxford was lost in his own world, completely focused on absorbing new science. Then, as if on cue, the kids heard a hissing and whirring sound in the distance.

"Listen!" Oxford grabbed Jazzi's arm. "Isn't that the same sound we heard on the beach?"

CHAPTER 9

STEP THIS WAY

The sound grew louder and louder. Jazzi's and Oxford's eyes zoomed in on a large, shadowy object that materialized from out of nowhere and glided majestically through the darkness up to the edge of the platform.

"Wow!" Jazzi turned toward Su—her jaw dropped open. "Is that it? Is that the cyber-thingy?"

He stood tall with head held high and proudly proclaimed, "That's it, Jazzi. That's your cyber-thingy!"

"Fascinating," said Oxford, squinting to get a sharper view. "It looks like a spaceship and high-tech rollercoaster combined into one."

"Yeah," Jazzi bit her lip, "…sort of."

Oxford snickered, knowing full well she didn't have a clue what he meant.

A ray of light flickered as silver-blue metallic doors rose up from the side of the coaster like giant wings. There were a total of six: two in the front car, two in the middle, and two in the back. The kids watched excitedly as a moving staircase descended onto the platform, preparing for new arrivals.

"C'mon, follow me." Su started to jump up onto the staircase.

"WAIT, wait, wait—not so fast!" Oxford took a step backward. "You expect me to get on? Just like that?"

"Oh, Oxy." Jazzi rolled her eyes in exasperation. "Now is not the time to wimp out."

"What, ya scared, Ox-man?" Su mocked.

"Not really, just make it a practice to avoid unnecessary risks."

"Relax. There've been no alien abductions reported to date. Look at me. I've traveled thousands of miles on the coaster, and I'm still in one piece."

"Apparently," Oxford muttered to himself.

"Could we hurry it up, guys?" Jazzi impatiently cut in. "Because not only will our parents be worried, Mr. Shawnly's going to freak if we turn

in our peace project late." She shook her head. "I've already got enough detentions to last me through college."

Su stepped aboard the moving staircase. "We're on cyber-time. You'll be home before anyone even notices you're gone."

"Cyber-time?" Jazzi repeated.

"It's complicated," he replied.

"Then maybe you should explain," Oxford insisted.

"I'll try," Su said arrogantly. "Time literally stands still when you're inside the coaster. That means you can virtually travel from one end of the earth to the other in no time at all. However the actual or real time depends on what part of the world you're in."

"I don't get it, Su." Jazzi scratched her head.

"I said it was complicated—but bottom line—you'll be home in time for dinner."

"That's a relief." Jazzi looked at Oxford. "One less thing to stress over."

Su ascended to the top of the staircase then stopped and looked down at Jazzi. "Did I forget to mention that once you're on board you're stuck— no turning back?" He grinned devilishly.

Jazzi loved a challenge so, with that, she shoved ahead of Oxford and jumped on. "So what are we waiting for?"

It was just like a mini version of the escalator in her favorite department store. Just riding on it made her nostalgic for the mall.

Oxford picked up Cat-Man-Doo and begrudgingly hopped on behind Jazzi. Nelson tagged confidently behind them.

The escalator had barely reached the top when Jazzi leaped inside the coaster.

"Wow," she gasped, "it looks like a spaceship in here." She gazed up and down the long narrow aisle that separated two rows of seats. At the front of the cabin was an enormous computerized control panel. There were various-sized remotes and switches and oversized tubes that glowed with waves of neon energy. Bright colored lights flashed on and off of large flat-screen monitors that lined the walls. And on the center screen was a huge world map with more menu options than you could possibly imagine. There was even an automatic pilot navigator on the console to keep the coaster from straying off course.

"You weren't exaggerating about this thing, Su." Jazzi jumped up and down, clapping her hands together. "Don't we need to wear some special space attire?"

"Not necessary," Su said as he removed Cat-Man-Doo's elastic cord. She wouldn't need it for the remainder of their journey.

"Why are we the only passengers, Su?" Oxford asked.

"You were my first stop, remember?"

"Oh." Oxford turned to Jazzi and whispered nervously in her ear. "So are we okay with being the *only* passengers?"

"Absolutely," she blurted. "We may have hit the jackpot. This could solve all my problems."

"Uh yeah," Oxford grumbled, "or create new ones."

"What? I can't hear you two back there," Su shouted.

Oxford quickly changed the subject. "Is the entire coaster computerized?"

"Of course, voice-activated too," Su called back. "It responds to all verbal commands."

"Too complex for me," Jazzi said.

"Trust me, guys," Su assured them. "It's all under my control."

That's what I'm afraid of, Oxford thought to himself.

Jazzi and Oxford took their seats while Nelson and Cat-Man-Doo curled up on nearby seats of their own.

"Sure hope the food's better than regular airline food," Jazzi said. "Peanuts and soda—yuck!"

"Actually, peanuts have been known to cause highly severe reactions in people with allergies, and we all know what sugar in soda can do . . ."

Jazzi let out a deep sigh. Oxford's oversized cranium was at it again.

". . . so of course airlines have put a halt on distribution to their customers for fear of . . ."

"Enough, Captain Factoid, I was just making conversation."

"Don't worry about food," Su shouted. "You'll receive a special one-a-day cyber-snack that is better than anything you've ever tasted. It meets all your daily nutritional requirements and will keep you energized and completely satisfied."

Oxford slumped back in his seat, slightly embarrassed. A bar automatically lowered over their laps, securing them in. Jazzi glanced up through the glass ceiling. "What a view."

Su nodded. "First class. Once you're moving its like being inside a whirling galaxy of underground shooting stars."

As the kids sat back enjoying the show, a small cabin door opened up revealing a new addition to the crew. It appeared to be a dwarfed robot or maybe the cyberite attendant that Su had mentioned.

"Welcome aboard. I am Hayley, your cyberite, and I will be monitoring all of your needs."

Hayley had a friendly smile accented by two tiny dimples on either side. Its small plump frame fit snugly inside a silver-blue uniform that shimmered whenever it moved. On its head sat a matching baseball cap with bold silver letters that read "Space Cadet."

Oxford poked Jazzi in the side. "That should be your hat."

Jazzi turned up her nose and simply ignored him. "That cyberite looks like a girl, if you ask me.

"Su said its non-gender."

"I know but, other than the hat, that outfit is something I would consider wearing if I had to wear a spacesuit."

Hayley was getting perturbed at Jazzi for not paying attention.

Oxford, unsure of what Hayley was capable of, immediately elbowed her. "Shhh, you need to listen, Jazzi."

Jazzi made a face and sat back in her seat with arms crossed.

Hayley smiled with appreciation and began the well-rehearsed speech. "Notice the bar has lowered over your laps, but for added safety, please fasten your seatbelts."

Jazzi and Oxford immediately complied.

"Always remain seated while the seatbelt sign is on, and turn off all electronic devices until otherwise notified. Also, remember to remain calm until you've reached your final destination—no matter what!"

Oxford looked alarmed. He nudged Jazzi and whispered, "No matter what?"

Hayley looked them directly in the eyes and said, "Get ready for the unknown!"

CHAPTER 10

JUST IMAGINE

As they waited for takeoff, Jazzi and Oxford felt like they were inside a 4-D movie. They could hear, smell, and feel things like never before. Bright vivid colors swirled in their heads, music sang in their ears, emotions grabbed at their hearts. It was all so intense.

"Hey Jazzi, where's our first stop?" Su called from the pilot's seat. "You're the navigator now."

Jazzi dug through her backpack and pulled out the old coffee-stained map Sir Sean had given her. As she carefully unfolded it and spread it out across her lap, she was surprised to see that the X was now resting over the country of England.

"That's weird," Jazzi said. "That's not where it was the last time I looked."

Suddenly Oxford's eyes got really huge. He extended his arm and slowly waved it back and forth across the map as if casting a spell. With a deep guttural sound he moaned, "Wooooo—the X—it's ALIVE!" A

50

menacing sneer consumed his face, causing his otherwise handsomely chiseled cheeks to distort into a freaky Friday-night-horror-show character.

Jazzi threw back her head in disgust. "Oxford—STOP it! Are you possessed or what? This is not the time to be pulling stupid pranks, you're too weird. I forgot Sir Sean said it might move so it took me by surprise, that's all." She looked down at the map and then up at Su. "It's on England, Su."

"England? Okay, that's a shortcut to New York, right Jazzi?" Su said jokingly.

"How should I know? That's just where the X is," she answered. "Wonder what's so special about England." She looked at Oxford assuming he was through messing with her and would offer up some intellectual insight.

"We'll soon find out," he replied smugly.

"That's weak," said Jazzi. "I had hoped for something a little more profound."

Oxford grinned and opened his notepad to post the news to the Kids' Worldwide Peace Club. Su punched in the coordinates while Jazzi sat back imagining the serene landscape of England: velvety green rolling hills, dotted with tall white castles, surrounded by fragrant flowers and lush gardens. *Hmmm, a young dreamy prince would be nice.* A sweet smile swept across Jazzi's face as her imagination ran wild, but she was quickly brought back to reality by the sound of Su's voice shouting out orders.

"Hang on!" Su commanded.

"AAAHHH!" screamed the kids. The CyberCoaster flew straight up from the platform like a dolphin out of water and then, just as quick, dropped back into a downward spiral—stomachs turned inside out and upside down.

"Ohhh," moaned Oxford. "What have we gotten ourselves into? I think I'm going to puke." He grabbed the cyber-sick bag, stuck his head inside and began to heave.

"GROSS!" Jazzi plugged her ears and buried her head as Oxford continued to hurl. Just thinking about it made her sick. "Can't you do something, Su?" she pleaded.

Su nodded and pressed a button on the keyboard so the CyberCoaster would level off. "Is that better?"

Oxford raised his head and gave Su a weak thumbs-up as the green slowly faded from his face. He grabbed a tissue to wipe his mouth and then proceeded to tell Jazzi he was sorry.

"Some warning would have been nice," she said, hoping to erase it from her memory.

"I'll try to remember that for next time," Oxford replied uncomfortably. He glanced around the coaster until he spotted Hayley, then motioned for assistance. "Excuse me, can I get an upgrade on this seat?"

Hayley patted Oxford on the head, slightly grinning, then marched to the back quarters.

"Oxford," Jazzi said, "you're embarrassing me."

"Well it can't hurt to ask. Thought it might not be so bumpy in another seat." He shifted from one cheek to the other trying to find a comfortable spot.

Su chuckled. "You'll get used to it."

The CyberCoaster slid through tunnels with lightning speed—twisting and turning with every curve. It was a sensation unlike anything they had ever experienced before. The bright lights from the stalactites and stalagmites shone down on them through the glass ceiling, creating a shimmer of colorful sparkles across their faces.

"Hold on. We're about to land," Su announced.

Jazzi lit up. "That was fast. This peace quest should take no time at all."

"Maybe for you," Oxford sighed.

It was just a matter of seconds before the coaster sailed around the last curve and came barreling in to a screeching halt. The outside doors flew up like monstrous wings. Hayley stood at the door waving goodbye as Su lead Jazzi and Oxford out onto the moving staircase. Nelson and Cat-Man-Doo jumped on behind, ready for the journey. When the trio arrived at the bottom of the platform they were once again fascinated by all the names on the wall. But the names were different now: Charlie Chaplin, Sir Winston Churchill, Charles Dickens, Robin Hood, and Annie were just a few that were artistically etched into the stone.

"Do you think it's Annie Oakley or Little Orphan Annie?" Jazzi asked as she traced over the names with her finger.

"Actually, Annie Oakley was strictly an American legend, Jazzi," Oxford reported all-knowingly, "and Little Orphan Annie is a cartoon character, so that presents a problem you see because . . ."

Su interrupted Oxford, "Hey, look over there." He pointed to an adjacent wall where a giant intricate mural of a yellow submarine was signed: John, Paul, George, and Ringo.

The kids walked over to get a closer view. "No way!" Jazzi said wide-eyed.

Oxford's jaw dropped. "I think my delectation just reached a whole new level."

"Huh?" Jazzi gave him a peculiar look. "Your *who* did *what*?"

"It means I'm delighted beyond expectation. I can't believe the Beatles were actually here." Oxford held his iNo up to Jazzi's face. "See?"

Irritated, she smacked his hand. "Get that thing away from me."

Oxford jerked his arm out of Jazzi's reach. "Hey, be careful! You almost made me drop it."

Su quickly intervened. "You know John Lennon wrote a song called *Imagine*."

"I love that song," Jazzi said. "You think John was searching for peace like us?"

"Uh-huh," said Su, "and I *imagine* he never found it."

As Su stood fixated on the fine details in the mural, Jazzi grabbed Oxford's arm and hurried him down the platform. Nelson and Cat-Man-Doo pranced close behind.

"Where are you taking me, Jazzi?"

"I don't know but there must be some way to exit this place. I'm feeling claustrophobic again."

Before Oxford had a chance to open his mouth, they could hear Su's voice echoing down through the tunnel—his words ricocheted off the walls.

"What do you two think you're doing?" Su's shouts grew louder the closer he got. "I told you to stay close to me or you'd wind up lost."

"Sorry, Su," Jazzi replied, "but there are so many nooks and crannies in these walls, I figured there must be a way out of here. I want to see what's above us and maybe soak up some warm rays. It's really damp down here and so stuffy and check out my hair," she stuck her bottom lip out, "it's starting to frizz!"

"It's not about you or your hair, Jazzi." Su spoke sternly. "I'm in charge here, but if you insist, go ahead and submit your picture now."

"Huh?" she said, perplexed. "My picture? What do you mean by that?"

Su moved in closer. "It means a picture of your face is going to end up on the side of a milk carton if you don't follow my instructions! Get it—M-I-A?"

"MIA? Missing in action! Wow, I didn't think about that." Jazzi felt bad. The last thing she wanted was to become a missing person. She just wanted some sunlight and fresh air, that's all.

"C'mon." Su shook his head. "Stay close to me." He turned and looked at Nelson and Cat-Man-Doo. "That goes for you too."

Immediately the group formed a single line and, like a platoon of soldiers, marched behind Su as instructed. They had almost reached the CyberCoaster when Su held up his hand and commanded them to stop. He approached a near-by wall where there appeared to be some kind of metal contraption tucked discreetly inside an alcove and pushed a small button. A door promptly opened and Su motioned to his four companions to follow him. Once inside, the doors slammed shut and they stood silently staring at each other—no questions asked.

Finally Jazzi couldn't take the silence any longer. "Somebody say something!" She blurted out.

"Okay," said Oxford. "What is this thing, Su?"

"It's a cyber-module and don't bother searching your iNo," Su said, still irritated, "you won't find it."

Oxford was taken aback.

"It's like an elevator—okay? It will lift us up to the surface. Isn't that what you wanted?"

Jazzi and Oxford nodded in unison.

Su pushed another button and said, "Then hold on, we're heading up!"

The module began humming and buzzing, then shot up like a rocket headed for the moon. The force of speed pushed their backs up against the wall so tightly they couldn't move. The intense turbulence sent Nelson's ears flapping back and forth like propellers—Cat-Man-Doo's fur ruffled up like she had been struck by lightning. Oxford clung on for dear life, his face once again turning a pale green. Jazzi closed her eyes hoping Oxford could keep everything down. There was no place to go if he were to get sick.

"Doesn't this thing have any straps to secure us in?" Oxford gasped. "I'm too young to die!"

"You really think you're going anywhere?" Su's voice quivered from the heavy vibrating. "You couldn't move if you tried."

That was Jazzi's fear. She stared up wide-eyed at the glass ceiling as they zoomed upward. It was like being on a thrill ride at an amusement park, minus the safety bar.

Oxford thought if he concentrated on the view he wouldn't feel nauseated, but all that changed once he looked up. His face suddenly went from pale green to stark white and panic overcame him as he watched the module heading straight for a wall of thick black mud.

"AAAHHH!" he screamed in terror. Jazzi couldn't speak. Oxford grabbed his companions' arms on either side and braced himself for impact. As the module rocketed closer and closer, he tried to prepare himself for the impending doom. Nelson's ears continued to flap uncontrollably as the module surged upward with lightning speed—Cat-Man-Doo closely resembled the bride of Frankenstein with her fur standing on end. But instead of crashing into a dirt death trap, as Oxford suspected, the module slipped right through the wall and came to a serene stop on solid ground. Silence abounded.

"Now, how easy was that?" Su grinned.

Oxford let out a deep sigh of relief, stunned by the whole ordeal. "No comment."

"Well, you might have at least warned us!" Jazzi was quite perturbed and nagged Su the whole way out the door until she realized something seemed strange. "Hey, it's dark outside and this can't be England, because it doesn't look anything like I imagined."

"Oh, we're in England alright, but let's just say we're exploring unfamiliar territory," Su answered vaguely.

"Unfamiliar territory?" Oxford frowned. "What's that supposed to mean?"

"You'll see," said Su.

CHAPTER 11

RAT-WHACK-A-RAMA

Once Jazzi and Oxford had calmed down after their earth-shattering ride, they decided it was best to listen to Su. When he motioned them to follow, they were going to follow. So off they went, trailing Su through the damp night air to an unknown destination. They had no idea what they were about to experience—they were just anxious to move on and see new sights. But instead of strolling across grassy green rolling hills, as Jazzi had hoped, they found themselves wandering through the heart of downtown London in the misty fog.

"So, Su," Jazzi gushed, "does this mean we get to experience London's night life, because I really love to dance, and since time stands still on the coaster, wouldn't that allow us plenty of time, although I'm not really dressed for it but . . . "

"Shhhhhh!" Oxford urged. "Relax, Jazzi."

Before Jazzi had completed her thought, Su had already pried open an old manhole cover and was waving them over.

"Can you do that?" Jazzi said.

"Do what?" Su looked back.

"Pry open a manhole cover and just crawl in? I mean, is it legal?"

"Didn't cross my mind," he replied. "C'mon."

Oxford arched his brow. "Are you seriously expecting Nelson and Cat-Man-Doo to follow us into that—that—disgusting hole in the pavement?"

Su nodded. "Not much choice unless they want to wait here."

"They better come," Oxford conceded.

"Hey, Su," Jazzi said, changing her tone, "is this a secret entrance to an underground dance club?"

"It's Plan B," Su replied rather strangely. "Stay close."

Oxford looked at Jazzi and lit up his iNo. "Check the map to make sure you read it right and this is actually where we're supposed to go."

Jazzi confirmed they were in the correct spot so they continued to do as Su had requested. Once inside the manhole they became painfully aware they were in an underground sewer somewhere beneath the busy streets of London. It took some time for their eyes to adjust to the dark. They could barely see anything other than black dingy walls that reeked of garbage and dead rodents. A cold damp fog drifted down into the sewer from street vents above, choking off what little fresh air there was.

"Yikes, it's disgusting down here, and the moisture is making my curls even frizzier!" Jazzi whined in Oxford's ear. "Hey," she ran her fingers through his hair, "the misty air seems to work for you. You look kinda cute with a droopy doo."

"This is no time to discuss hair, Jazzi." Oxford pushed her hand away and turned to Su. "If this is your idea of Plan B, I'd sure hate to see the other options."

"Listen," Jazzi whispered. "I hear something."

"Me too," Oxford replied. "Sounds like Big Ben."

Jazzi tilted her head. "Who?"

"Big Ben, the famous London clock," Oxford replied.

High above them they heard a loud bong-bonging that echoed through the sewers like a boom box. It was very eerie, like something out of an old Dickens novel.

"Hmmm, midnight already?" Oxford looked at Jazzi, stumped. "Let's see, if London is nine hours ahead, then it's only three p.m. at home."

"So that's good news, right? I mean we might actually be able to gain time which would extend our spring break," Jazzi said, delighted.

Oxford nodded. "Impressive."

"Cyber-time, guys," Su reminded them. "It doesn't matter what the clock says. Think of yourselves as being in a time warp. Time doesn't matter, although my cell phone is accurate if you should get curious."

Jazzi groaned. "Then does that mean we're ahead or behind schedule?"

Oxford shrugged. "Just go with it, Jazzi."

As their eyes adjusted to the darkness, they were startled to discover dozens of other eyes staring back at them. It was strange because all of the eyes were dark except for one pair of very intense blue. They seemed to be following Jazzi's every move.

"Su," Jazzi said nervous, "is there some sort of life-form down here?"

"Maybe. Stay close in case."

"In case of what?" Oxford gulped.

"Well . . ." Su hesitated.

"Well nothing!" Jazzi whispered fiercely. "I need answers and I need them now!"

Jazzi grabbed Oxford's arm in alarm.

Suddenly Big Ben stopped booming and it became deathly quiet; that is, all except for a strange shuffling noise accompanied by some weird rattling.

Seconds later a band of young boys emerged from the hidden corners and alcoves in the walls. Their skin was pasty white, and their clothes were torn and mismatched.

Several of them circled around the trio and then began to close in. The hair on Nelson's back bristled as he growled and bared his teeth. Cat-Man-Doo hissed and arched her back, trying to ward off an imminent attack.

Just then the leader of the pack grabbed Jazzi's arm.

She shrieked, "Let go of me, you—you—FREAK!"

He merely peered at her. "Ar you Jazzi?" asked the pale-skinned boy in his thick English accent.

"Am I Jazzi? Am I JAZZI?" she screamed, swinging her arms wildly in all directions. "A better question is who are *you* and how do you know my name?"

"Didn't mean ta scare ya, mate," the boy said nicely, "jus thot Su mus 'ave told you bou' us. We don' get many visitors down 'ere."

"I can see why!" She threw an angry look at Su. "You don't, by chance, happen to have any air freshener—do you? It's really stinky!"

Jazzi's face turned a bright red as she struggled to keep from breathing in the rancid sewer smells.

"Try breathin' thru ya mouth, Jazz—it's a bi' easier," suggested another even paler boy.

"It's Jazzi—NOT Jazz!" she snapped.

Oxford pulled a tissue from his back pocket and covered his nose as he stepped out of the way of the gang leader. He seemed to be pushing a scrappy-looking boy forward.

"This is 'Enery, our elected represen'ive to ya kids' peace club," he said.

'Enery gave a slight wave. He was wearing a wrinkled brown tweed jacket over a pair of well-worn jeans. A flat cap sat on top of his head, and under his left arm was a wooden crutch. His left leg was slightly shorter than his right.

"Don' be concerned bou' 'Enery's 'andicap," the leader said, "ee's one mean ra' whackah."

"Did I hear that right?" Oxford looked alarmed. "Did you say *rat whacker*—meaning rat as in—rodent?"

Jazzi leaned into Oxford's ear. "How did that 'Enery kid become our representative?"

Oxford stood dumbfounded. "Maybe he saw the message I posted—ask him."

Before the boy could answer, a loud commotion came from farther down the sewer. Barking, howling, snarling—all sorts of hullabaloo!

"Quick! Let's go see wha' the troubl' is," the boy cried out.

Together, the group ran down through the sewer, hopping over spilled garbage and assorted debris.

"Eweee!" Jazzi wailed, slipping on an old brown banana peel. "It smells worse than the cafeteria dumpster."

They continued running toward the ruckus as fast as they could when suddenly the leader threw out his arm, causing a domino effect as they all went crashing into each other.

"Wouldn't it have been easier to yell STOP?" Jazzi picked herself up, yanking rotten debris from her hair.

"Brilliant, Jazzi, why didn't I think uv tha'?" the leader joked back sarcastically.

"Look—over there!" Su pointed. Nelson was crouched in the corner bearing his teeth, facing off with a giant snarling rat he had pinned up against the wall. All the growling and barking, mixed with Cat-Man-Doo's hissing, was stirring up quite a scene.

"Be bloody careful," one of the boys cautioned, "your mutt is no match for tha' ra'. It would jus' as soon serve 'em up wif afer'noon tea—the cat too."

In no time at all Nelson was surrounded by a swarm of rats: big nasty ones with long pointy, razor-sharp teeth and foot-long tails. They were everywhere!

'Enery decided it was time for action. "Ou'ta ma way!" he yelled. He swung his crutch wildly above his head: rats went flying in every direction. One skimmed Oxford's arm as it sailed past him and, once again, he was sent into a near state of panic.

"AAAHHH, I'm outta here!" he screamed and started running back in the other direction. "Hang onto the map, Jazzeeeeee!" His voice faded as he sprinted for the exit.

"What about 'Enery?" Jazzi asked, turning to Su for direction. "He thinks he's our representative."

"Bring him," he replied, "we're gonna need that rat-whacker to get out of here alive!"

CHAPTER 12

JUST WHEN YOU LEAST EXPECT IT!

Jazzi and Su sprinted back to the entrance of the sewer, with 'Enery hobbling close behind. When they met up with Oxford, he was beside himself, trying desperately to pry open the manhole cover. 'Enery stepped up to assist him and, along with the help of the other boys, managed to lift it up. Once the cover was open, Oxford helped Nelson and Cat-Man-Doo paw their way back up to the surface. Jazzi and Oxford tumbled out onto the street after them, while Su stayed below to help boost 'Enery up. Once they were all on top, Su slammed the cover shut. Nelson led the way back to the CyberCoaster barking, along with Cat-Man-Doo who continued to hiss at the squealing and scratching sounds still ringing in the night air. It seemed like an eternity before they arrived back to the CyberCoaster—they were filthy dirty and exhausted from running.

"Whew, I can't believe we made it!" Jazzi panted with relief as she fell back into her seat. "What about the other boys, 'Enery? Will they be alright?"

'Enery took a seat across the aisle from Jazzi and petted Nelson on the head. "Good job, ol' chap." He turned to Jazzi. "The otha' blokes are countin' on me ta find 'em some peace."

"Guess they could use some living the way they do," Jazzi agreed. "Hey 'Enery, who was the person hiding in the corner with the blue eyes? They kept following me everywhere I moved, but I never saw who they belonged to."

"Nah, don't know any blue-eyed blokes, musta ben yer 'magination," he replied.

Jazzi nodded, she tended to agree knowing her imagination could get carried away at times. Still, they really stood out in the dark sewer.

"Su," Oxford called out, scratching his head confused, "that was creepy. A filthy rodent filled sewer is the last place I expected to end up in."

Su had nothing to say. He sat staring vacantly up through the glass ceiling.

"Su?" Oxford tried to get his attention again.

"Huh? What did you say, Oxford?"

"I was just commenting on how scary the sewer was and kind of wondering why you didn't warn us ahead of time?"

"You had to experience it for yourself," Su argued.

"What?" Oxford sat straight up in his seat. "We could have *died* down there or at best, contracted some rare rodent-infested disease!"

"But you didn't," Su replied sternly.

Before Oxford could argue his point, Hayley stuck a cyber-snack between his lips. It really hit the spot after their long grueling ordeal. "Shower?" He looked up at the cyberite grinning; his white teeth looked even whiter against his dirt-smudged face.

Hayley handed him a spray can of cyber-disinfectant and told him to spray his entire body from head to toe; clothes and all. It was better than a shower and they needed to conserve their water supply. It also acted as toothpaste so he could spray it inside his mouth. He took it hesitantly, but was pleased with the results. He actually felt like a new kid.

Su's attitude was becoming more and more irritating to Oxford, but rather than trying to figure him out, he decided to join in conversation with Jazzi and their new traveling companion.

"How's that sewer life working for ya, 'Enery?" Oxford began. "It's pretty nasty down there."

"Don' 'ave a choice," he answered.

"Where's your family?" Jazzi asked.

"Me mum n' me pop were both kill'd in an auto acciden'. I jus' hurt ma' leg." He pointed with his crutch. "I was sen' to an orphanage, but ran away."

"How come?" asked Jazzi.

"Bahhh—too many rules," he said.

Jazzi understood, she wasn't a fan of rules herself.

Oxford listened intently as 'Enery shared his past.

"Actually," 'Enery went on, "da sewa's nah all tha' bad once ya ge' use to it."

"You can get used to it?" Jazzi wrinkled up her nose.

"Yeh, but I do miss 'avin a gud meal n' sof' place ta res' ma noggin."

"A little fresh air would be nice," Jazzi added.

"How'd you find our website?" Oxford jumped in. "Do you have access to a computer at school?"

"One of da blokes foun' an ol' laptop n' 'ooked it up ou'side a pub in da back alley—that's our school."

Jazzi was impressed. "Clever—right Oxy?"

"Definitely," he agreed.

"It lets us stay n' touch wif Su n' dats 'ow we found you."

Jazzi rubbed her chin, curious.

"Wait—you mean Su knew you and the other boys were living in the sewers all along and didn't tell us?"

"A small detail he forgot, Jazzi," Oxford said, displeased.

"Is that true, Su?" she shouted. "Because you said to trust you!"

"As you should." Su grinned mischievously. "Had you trusted me by following my rules instead of running off like you did when we first landed, we would have entered into England according to plan A."

"There actually was a plan A?" Oxford asked.

"Of course there was. We could have avoided the sewer experience all together. Plan A was to have 'Enery meet us above ground during daylight hours. You might have seen England the way you had hoped, Jazzi, but then you would have missed out on seeing another side of life—a life you would have never imagined."

Su was right, she would have never known sewer life existed had she not seen it for herself. She had so much to learn.

Oxford turned and pointed his finger at Jazzi. "One of these days you're going to realize that following the rules is a good thing!"

She gave Su and Oxford a look of disgust. "I'll let you know when that time comes." She turned back to 'Enery. "Sorry for the interruption, please finish your story."

"Wen I learnt Su was researchin' peace for a school project I wan'ed ta join in. Lord knows I cud use some in ma own life—survivin' ain't been easy. A lil' bit o' peace mite 'elp fill da hole in ma 'eart, but for now—it's all bloody good." 'Enery smiled.

"I wonder." A look of sadness swept across Jazzi's face.

"You're not the only one who could use some peace, 'Enery." Oxford said, raising his voice so Su would hear.

Su was just about to respond to Oxford's remark when Jazzi chimed in. "You know you were wrong not to tell us about 'Enery and the sewer, Su."

"Maybe, but then you wouldn't have wanted to go. When you said the X was over England, I decided to take advantage of it. I recently met 'Enery in a chat room and was curious about his life in the sewer. Thought we could pick up some material for the peace project, but I wasn't planning on going inside the sewer, until you decided to do things your way. You just gave me the excuse I needed to switch to plan B."

Jazzi frowned. "That's where we disagree."

"But you have to admit that the sewer lifestyle was enlightening, you met some interesting new friends, and no one was harmed in the process. Ready for more surprises?"

"Preferably peaceful ones," Oxford agreed.

Jazzi crossed her arms and sat back in her seat troubled. She knew it was better to keep her mouth shut and listen to Su. After-all, he played a key role in completing the peace assignment. She got up and moved across the aisle next to 'Enery and asked him to help her find their next stop.

After they finished scanning the map, Jazzi looked up. "Guess where the X is now, Su?"

"Why don't you just tell me, Jazzi."

"Did it find its way to a less stressful area?" Oxford grunted.

Hayley snickered from the back of the cabin and went about feeding Nelson and Cat-Man-Doo their cyber-pet snacks. Nothing ever surprised a cyberite.

"It's Switzerland!" She turned to 'Enery. "Have you ever been to Switzerland?"

'Enery beamed. "Nah, but I've always wan'ed to go there evah since I read 'bout it in a book."

"*Heidi*?" Jazzi asked, realizing that was the only thing Swiss she knew besides cheese.

"Uh-huh, I remembah thinkin' da Alps mus' be so peaceful."

Jazzi nodded. "Well, we'll soon find out."

Su downloaded "Switzerland" into the program and yelled for everyone to get ready for takeoff."

Oxford logged on to the Kids' Worldwide Peace Club website and posted their ETA, while the others prepared for another wild ride. Off they went, forging their way through the most eye-popping terrain they had ever seen. 'Enery was having the time of his life, while Oxford, on the other hand, grabbed for the cyber sick bag. Would he ever get used to the ups and downs of cyber- cruising?

CHAPTER 13
ICEBERG WEDGIE

I n the blink of an eye Hayley was darting about the cabin, preparing for landing, and no one was more thrilled than Oxford. When his stomach was happy, he was happy. As the kids began exiting down the platform, they noticed there were not only names carved in the walls: Carl Jung, Wilhelm Tell, Heidi and Grandfather, among others, there was also a large "Welcome to Switzerland" banner.

The group stepped into the module where they were instantly transported to the surface. Bright sunshine flooded over them as they set foot onto the snowy white terrain.

"I can barely see," Jazzi complained, squinting from the glare. "Where is everyone?"

As Jazzi struggled to get her bearings, she barely noticed a group of kids waving their arms excitedly in the air. "Here we are! Here we are! We got your e-mail and have been waiting anxiously for your arrival."

In the distance, you could see kids herding goats over silvery glistening hillsides and across the valley, sounds of yodeling echoed from mountaintop to mountaintop.

"Now this is what I call peaceful." Jazzi smiled at Oxford, but he wasn't paying any attention to her. He was too busy wandering about the hillside searching for a Wi-Fi signal.

She frowned. "Are you listening to me, Oxy?"

"What? Oh, uh, sorry—sorta busy right now."

"Yeah, well, quit messing with your stupid iNo."

"But you don't understand, Jazzi, I've got a weak signal." He paused to wipe a snow flurry from his glasses. "If I don't stay connected to the network, we won't be able to communicate with anyone."

But as Oxford struggled to defend his actions, silent sound waves emitted from his iNo, resonating deep down below the fresh fallen snow. The intense vibrations from his communications device triggered an abrupt reaction inside the mountain, resulting in a huge explosion of activity and chaos.

"What's going on?" Jazzi screamed. "I was just going to say that maybe this is where we'll find peace, but . . ."

Before she could finish her thought, her words were drowned out by the sound of galloping hooves flying along the trails.

The kids whirled around just in time to see dozens of goats heading straight toward them. Behind the goats an avalanche of snow roared down the mountain with lightning speed.

"RUN!" a cry echoed in the background.

"Uh-oh." Oxford cringed. "I think I may have accidentally caused a slight underground disturbance . . ."

Jazzi glared. "What's that supposed to mean?"

"Well, ya see, ummm, how can I put this delicately…?" Oxford extended his arm and looked directly into her eyes. "Grab on and RUN! Jazzi gasped and grabbed onto Oxford's arm, along with 'Enery and Su. Clinging together for their lives, they ran down the mountain as fast as they could. Nelson and Cat-Man-Doo were right on their heels.

They had almost made it to safety when a gigantic wall of snow overtook them, smashing them face first to the ground. There they were, flat on their faces, pressed to the earth, freezing like snow cones at the fair.

A moment of silence gave way to gasps for air as Jazzi desperately fought her way to the surface. "Wow!" she coughed and choked, "that wasn't in the plan." Once she regained the feeling back in her fingers, she proudly waved the map as far above her head as her arm would extend.

"It's safe!" she yelled proudly. "Told you I wouldn't lose it, Oxy!" She was hoping for a shout or two of praise but there was no response. "Oxy?" Slowly she turned her head from side to side. "Hey—where is everyone?"

"Over here, Jazzi!" Su and 'Enery lifted their arms to affirm they were both alive.

"Where's Oxy?" Jazzi looked around. "Oxy, where are you? Tell me you aren't still playing with your stupid iNo!"

"No!" 'Enery cried out. "Over there! Nelson is sniffing and digging around in the snow. I think Oxford might be in trouble!"

The kids pulled themselves out from under the pile of snow and stood watching nervously as Nelson dug frantically, trying to find Oxford. Cat-Man-Doo sat shivering by his side. A faint muffled cry resounded from under the mound of snow. Nelson began digging faster and faster, but still no sign.

"He must be trapped!" Su shouted. "We've got to act fast or he'll freeze to death!"

"I'll try to find a shovel." Jazzi ran off in the direction of a nearby chalet.

"There's no time!" said 'Enery. He turned his crutch upside down and started shoveling with the handle.

Su marveled. "You work that crutch like a pro."

Little by little, faint cries grew louder. Soon Jazzi came running back, panting and out of breath. Accompanying her was a new helper, dragging a shovel behind him.

"Hi—outta my way!" said the boy. "I'm Finn, but no time for intros. We've got to work fast if you want to see your friend again."

Finn dove in with his shovel, and before long, a crop of bright red hair poked through the white snow. Seconds later, Oxford popped up like a puppet in a wind-up music box—his cheeks bulging with snow.

"What hit me?" he asked, spitting out a mouthful of melted ice.

Finn held out his hand for support and helped Oxford to his feet.

As he stood there swaying dizzily from side to side, a group of kids gathered around him cheering.

Jazzi poured him a cup of warm hot chocolate from Finn's thermos. "Are you okay, Oxy?"

"I dunno," he rubbed his head, "just when you think you've found peace—an avalanche hits."

"Profound," Finn responded.

"Spot on," 'Enery nodded.

"Yeah, deep." Su snickered sarcastically.

The kids circled together around Oxford, huddling up close to keep him warm. But when he reached inside his pocket for his iNo, he started to hyperventilate.

"Oh no—OH NO! MY iNo! Where's my iNo?"

Instantly he dropped his mug of hot chocolate and fell to his knees, grabbing Su's arm on the way down. The group watched as he crawled around, scooping up snow in his hands, letting out occasional whimpers until his frozen fingers finally brushed up against something hard.

"Oh thank goodness!" he cried with glee. "I found it—I FOUND IT!"

The group was stunned by Oxford's reaction.

"Geez, Oxy, it's just your iNo." Jazzi rolled her eyes.

Oxford looked up, offended. "You know this is our only connection to the website, Jazzi, and without it we would have no way to complete our assignment."

"Forget it, man," Su heckled. "Your iNo is toast—it's all wet!"

Oxford let go of Su's arm, disgusted by his remark. He stood up on his feet, cradling his iNo with both hands. He gently brushed off the snow and, clutching it tightly to his chest, turned toward Su and said, "Do you really think the elements of nature could destroy a device with such technological magnitude? It's waterproof up to 300 feet below sea level." And with that he turned his back on Su.

"Wow!" Jazzi concluded. "You're way too attached to that thing!"

Oxford turned his head and started talking about the landscape, hoping to divert the conversation away from his iNo. "This is a very scenic area we're in but…," he rubbed his eyes and looked at Jazzi, "… where *are* we?"

"Really, Oxy?" she replied. "You seriously don't remember we're in Switzerland?"

"Oh yeah, right, right, it's slowly coming back to me—CyberCoaster, Kids' Peace Club, United Nations—I remember now."

"That's great and I'm sure you also remember we've got a task to complete. Let me introduce you to Finn."

"Who?"

"Finn," Jazzi repeated.

"He looks familiar." Oxford reached out to shake his hand.

"Umm, maybe that's because he just rescued you?" Jazzi was losing patience.

"Oh, yeah—heh, heh." Oxford looked away, embarrassed.

"You know, Oxy, it was odd because some stranger at the lodge gave Finn the shovel before I even got there, and told him he was going to make a good representative," said Jazzi. "How did he know I needed a shovel— or a representative?" She rubbed her cold hands together, puzzled.

"Maybe you should ask him," Oxford commented.

"I'm not stupid," Finn said he'd never seen him before. He had really kind blue eyes though—it was like we had met before. But what does it matter? He only helped save your life."

Oxford stood pondering Jazzi's words. It would have been nice to be able to thank the man. Oh well—it was too late to go hunt him down now.

Finn picked up his shovel and gave a thumbs-up.

Oxford looked the boy up and down. "Nice pants," he said with a shiver.

Finn wore traditional lederhosen pants with embroidered suspenders. "My father insists," he explained. "He is very stubborn and believes 'the old ways are the only ways'. He won't ever give me a chance to voice my own opinion," Finn sighed. "This is not a peaceful way to live and first chance I get," he fidgeted with the seat of his pants, "I'm losing these lame lederhosen."

"Really?" Jazzi replied. "I think they're cute."

"Cute? Well, you can have 'em—wedgies and all!"

Jazzi snickered. "Gotcha, fidgety Finn, but save shopping for another day. You need to go grab your things and say your goodbyes."

Finn ran off to get his belongings. It wasn't long before he had returned, excited to be joining the group. Once they were all inside the coaster, Hayley was right there to make sure everyone was comfortable and secure for takeoff. Su called back to Jazzi and inquired about their next location. She quickly pulled out the map and began searching for the X.

Su waited patiently, knowing it could be anywhere. He called out a second time. "Am I sensing a problem, Jazzi?"

CHAPTER 14

THE SOLE MAN

N ope, found it. Says we're to go to Holland—the Netherlands."

"Holland it is." Su pushed the lever and off they went. In no time at all they had landed and were making their way down the coaster's ramp. Jazzi was first to reach the wall and read the names out loud.

"Rembrandt, Vincent Van Gogh, Paul Gauguin, Anne Frank...," Jazzi paused. "Anne Frank, that name's familiar. Wasn't she . . ."

". . . a young Jewish girl who wanted peace more than anything?" Oxford stepped in. "Yes she was. Remember Jazzi, we learned about her in history. She kept a diary that was later made into a book."

"Oh yeah, history—*borrr*ing! Refresh my memory, did she ever find peace?"

Oxford lowered his head sorrowfully.

Jazzi was becoming more and more aware of the challenges that lay ahead. She glanced around the station and, despite Su's rules, noticed a light at the end of the tunnel and set off on her own to see what it was.

Before long she stumbled upon a small shoe shop. Oddly enough it was shaped like a giant boot. Above it hung a sign that read: "Shoes Repaired While You Wait or New Ones If You Won't."

Now that's a strange name for a shoe shop, Jazzi thought to herself. Intrigued by the name, she decided to step through the doorway and satisfy her curiosity. Secretly she was hoping to find some fancy foreign designer shoes, but once inside she couldn't believe her eyes. It was like being inside a giant boot. She rubbed her hand against the shop's smooth buckskin walls— there was no mistaking the sweet smell of leather. As Jazzi bounced across a thick cushiony rug she was startled by the sound of someone clearing his throat.

"Uh-hmm . . ." uttered a voice.

Jazzi whirled around. There, sitting behind the counter, was a peculiar old cobbler whittling away at a pair of wooden shoes. His kind blue eyes sparkled against his rosy cheeks, highlighting his neatly trimmed silver beard and matching mullet hairstyle. Over his black turtleneck sweater, he wore a purple and white pin-striped vest. On his head, tilted to the side, sat a funny-looking cone-shaped hat that trailed down over one shoulder.

"Are you enjoying your search, Jazzi?"

"Well, it's challenging, but—hey!" She stopped. "How do you know my name?"

The cobbler chuckled. "You're searching for something, aren't you?"

"Yes, but—what are you? A shoe-man or a mind-reader?"

"I'm a cobbler by trade, but around here, I'm known as the *soul man*."

Jazzi watched perplexed as the man slipped on a pair of dark glasses, grabbed a shoe, and began singing, "Yeah, I'm a *soooul* man . . . !" He quickly spun around, wailing into his shoe as if it were a microphone.

Jazzi stared at him blankly, unsure of what to say next. "Um, you must get pretty bored down here."

"Me? Nah." He picked up a rag and wiped the sweat from his brow. "I have lots of work to do. Creating a pair of shoes is not an easy job, you know."

"I never gave it much thought," she said dismissively.

"Oh my, how sad."

"Sad?" She tilted her head to one side.

"Picture in your mind all the different sizes, shapes, and colors there are."

Jazzi thought of all the shoes in her closet.

"And even though shoes may look different on the outside, the insides have many similarities—just like people."

Jazzi wrinkled her nose, puzzled. "And you think shoes are like people—*why*?"

He smiled. "They protect souls."

"People's souls?"

He nodded. "I repair the holes."

"So you fix soles that have holes?"

"A soul is not whole until it's healed."

"But how do you heel a sole with a hole?"

"Replace the missing peace."

Jazzi frowned, trying to make sense of their conversation.

"One peace can fill a whole soul and if you pick the *right* one it will last forever."

"You mean it will *never* wear out?"

He gave a slight nod. "Says so right here." He pointed to an open black book lying on the edge of the counter. "See? Guaranteed to last an eternity."

Jazzi shook her head, confused. "Whose book is that?"

"Anyone who wants to read it."

"Anyone?"

"Of course. It's like an instruction manual with directions."

"Directions? Like a map?" She patted her pocket, making sure the map was secure.

"No," he paused, "it's more like instructions on finding your direction."

"Stop—*please*!" Jazzi grabbed her ears. "I can't take anymore! Can't you just talk like a normal person? Do you fix holes in people's soles, or do you heal souls that need to be whole?"

He listened compassionately.

"And…and…," she raised her hand to her forehead, frustrated, "do you mean one *piece* or one *peace*?"

"Don't fret, young lady." The cobbler patted her gently on the shoulder. "If you seek it, you will find it."

Jazzi was at a loss for words. What did he mean? Seek *what*? Find *what*? It was all so confusing, yet the eccentric old man seemed wise in an odd sort of way, and for a fleeting moment, she had a crazy notion he might be able to help her. She wasn't sure how—she just knew that deep down inside she felt empty and was fairly certain it had nothing to do with the soles of her shoes. Trying to figure out what the old cobbler actually meant had Jazzi's head spinning. Yet, at the same time, he was so intriguing she couldn't take her eyes off of him. She watched mesmerized as he danced gaily over to his armchair and plopped himself down. With both hands he gripped the arms of the chair and wiggled back and forth into the overstuffed feather cushion until it felt just so

"Are we still talking about shoes?" Jazzi raised an eyebrow.

He gave her a quick little wink and, with smiling blue eyes, leaned back and pulled a lever on the side of his chair. "Go in peace!"

"Wait! Where are you going? Please don't leave—I still have questions!" All at once Jazzi fell back against the wall in horror. From out of nowhere a giant pink tongue dropped from the ceiling and rolled out onto the floor like a carpet, swallowing up the cobbler and his chair with one big, juicy slurp!

"AHHHHHH!" She held her head and ran screaming outside the shop and straight into Oxford. He had gone looking for her and was standing outside in front of the store window admiring the craftsmanship of the shoes.

"OW!" he cried out. "Look where you're going, Jazzi!"

"Oxy—OXY—what are you doing here? Did you see that? Where did he go?"

He frowned. "See what? Where did *who* go?"

"The sole-man, or soul-man—I DON'T KNOW!" Jazzi was so frustrated she was ready to pull her hair out.

"The sole-man? Don't you mean the cobbler or perhaps—shoe-man?"

Jazzi shook her head wildly. "I mean the man who repairs holes in people's soles, or, I'm not sure, maybe it's that he makes people's souls whole! I don't know what his title is," she threw out her arms frustrated, "and what difference does it make anyways, because now he's GONE!"

Oxford leaned closer. "Gone—as in *dead* gone?"

"No—well, maybe—who knows? All I know is that he was sitting in his chair talking to me one minute and the next minute he wasn't!"

"But you must have seen him leave." Oxford was stumped.

"NO, he didn't leave—a gigantic pink tongue unraveled from the ceiling and slurped him up like an afternoon snack!"

"WHAT? You say you saw an *actual* tongue?" Oxford was speechless.

"YES, how many times do I have to tell you? The tongue inside the shoe shop. It was so gross!" She grabbed onto Oxford shivering.

"That's hideous!" Oxford said, disgusted.

"Uh-huh! It was a nasty pink color with millions of lumpy little bumps all over it." Jazzi stuck out her own tongue to make a point.

"Lumpy bumps—are you sure? Try to calm down, Jazzi." Oxford patted her on the shoulder. "Your eyes must be playing tricks on you. I bet you're just tired."

Oxford was really getting on Jazzi's nerves. "Look, I know what I saw!" Her heart began to race as she fumbled for a place to sit down and catch her breath.

Oxford reached over and put his hand over her mouth trying to quiet her down. "Focus, Jazzi. Take a long deep breath and let it out slowly."

Jazzi shoved his hand away, irked. "How am I supposed to breathe with your hand over my mouth?"

"Just trying to help." Oxford slowly moved away, suggesting they better get back to the group.

Jazzi closed her eyes and took another deep breath. "Okay, I feel better now and you're right."

"I am?" Oxford was taken aback. "*That's a first!*" he thought to himself.

"Yes, you're right. We need to get back because we've been gone far too long. Su's going to wonder where we are and what we were doing and I'm in no mood to be interrogated by him or anyone else. We'll just keep this little episode between the two of us, okay, Oxy?"

There was no reply.

Jazzi pinched his elbow. "I said, OKAY?"

"What? Oh—yeah, sure. Hearing *you* tell me I was right threw me for a loop. I wanted to linger in the moment."

"Oh, stop your nonsense, we need to get out of here."

Oxford trailed Jazzi as they ran off together to meet up with the group. As they neared their destination, they could see Su leaning up against the module with his arms crossed, tapping his foot.

"Hello." Jazzi smiled uncomfortably. "Got distracted by some shoes and sort of lost track of time—heh, heh."

Su returned a slightly irritated smile and held his arm out. "After you," he said, pointing to the entrance of the module. "Everyone is inside, patiently waiting. They'll be pleased to see you."

Jazzi grinned sheepishly as she and Oxford stepped inside. No one bothered to question their late arrival—they politely squeezed together to make room. Jazzi leaned her back against the module wall and sighed.

"It's okay," Oxford said, trying to console her. "This peace project has you wound up. Things are bound to get better."

"You think so?" She turned to Oxford with a serious expression. "You really didn't see anything strange in the shoe shop?"

CHAPTER 15

LURKING IN THE TULIPS

C 'mon, Jazzi." Oxford nudged her. "You've got to forget about the shoe shop and whatever it was you thought you saw."

"Don't tell me what to do!" She raised her voice. "I know what I saw."

He squeezed her hand, hoping she would settle back and enjoy the journey, but as much as she wanted to, she simply couldn't relax. The image of a giant sized tongue swallowing up a strange old cobbler would possibly be embedded in her memory forever. And his words—*seek it and you will find it*—kept popping up inside her head like a flashing neon sign.

Jazzi's mind continued to wander even after the module had surfaced but, once the door opened, her thoughts drifted elsewhere. There, unveiled before her eyes like a priceless piece of art, was one of the most spectacular sights she had ever seen. A field of brightly colored tulips, surrounded by clusters of kids, stood bunched together like fresh bouquets of flowers. It was hard to tell where the flowers stopped and the kids began.

"Now that's what I call peaceful," Oxford sighed, caressing his iNo.

Nelson barked, as if agreeing. He and Cat-Man-Doo felt confined in the coaster and could hardly wait to go romping through the fields.

"It appears peaceful all right—maybe a little *too peaceful?*" Jazzi noted skeptically. "Let's go find our next representative."

Everyone agreed with Jazzi and decided to scatter in different directions, eager to learn more about their peers. As they walked across the meadow they observed children laughing and frolicking in the fields, but the peace was soon shattered by the sound of loud barking off in the distance.

"Now what?" Jazzi threw up her arms, irritated.

"It sounds like Nelson," Oxford said. "Hurry, we can network later."

Jazzi and Oxford went running off across the field to see what the fuss was, hoping it was nothing more than dog play. But when they arrived, they couldn't believe their eyes! It was Nelson alright—dangling from a tree—struggling to free himself from the grip of a huge boa constrictor. And, as if that weren't shocking enough, the creature was wearing dark glasses. Despite the fact the colorfully coiled serpent couldn't see, it had methodically slithered its way through the thick flower fields, thanks to the aide of one tiny wiener dog. Yet this was no *ordinary* wiener dog. This was a bona fide, highfalutin, seeing-eye wiener dog with a top hat on its head and a shiny gold monocle adorning its left eye. To and fro he went, frantically tapping his miniature cane on the snakes back, navigating every move.

The kids gazed up befuddled as the wiener dog peered down and politely tipped his top hat. "Good day, young explorers. I am Nafferton and this . . ." he pointed his cane at his slinky companion, "is my boss, Pookie."

"POOKIE?" Jazzi's mouth dropped open. "You call that monster Pookie?"

Oxford's jaw fell on the ground. "A…a…*talking* wiener dog?"

"This is worse than I thought!" Jazzi dropped to her knees, pleading for help. "Somebody do something! Anything—HURRY!"

Cat-Man-Doo peeked through the branches of a nearby bush, mute with fear.

"That's the biggest snake I've ever seen!" 'Enery looked down at his rat-whacker, discouraged.

"It's a b-b-boa constrictor," Finn stuttered, "but how did Nelson wind up in its jaws?"

Oxford stood tongue-tied, not uttering a sound.

"An enormous reptile that's completely dependent on a tiny wiener dog to control its entire future?" Su beamed. "Sweet!"

"How can you be so insensitive, Su?" Jazzi yelled angrily. "What about Nelson?"

"Well, you've got to admit, it's a rather odd pair."

"I don't need *more odd* in my life, I *need* Nelson!"

Jazzi rose back up on her feet, beside herself, she didn't know what to do. The sparkling rays of sunlight that, only a short time before, had warmed her face, were now being overshadowed by clouds of worry. She stood staring up at Nelson, too nervous to breathe, when she had a sudden urge to turn around. Peering out from behind a tree, a pair of smiling blue eyes winked at her, then dashed off into the flower fields.

"Did you see that?" A shiver ran up Jazzi's spine.

"See what?" Su replied. "I can't take my eyes off the odd couple—it's fascinating."

"Oh never mind," she said, folding her arms agitated. "It's just that everywhere I go I see a pair of blue eyes staring back at me. I don't get it—is someone playing tricks on me?"

"Maybe," Su agreed, "But there are no tricks when it comes to the simple law of nature." Su was rather enjoying messing with her head.

Jazzi huffed. "What's that supposed to mean?"

"You know, the law of nature—animals survive by feeding off each other. I'd say having a boa around your neck puts Nelson is in a precarious position."

"If this is your way of making me feel better, Su, it's not working!" Jazzi shrieked and rubbed her temples. "You're giving me a headache."

Su smirked. "It's a real shame because there's no way Nelson could have seen the creature. It blends in so nicely with the flowers and surrounding foliage. It was probably slithering through the fields searching for an unsuspecting victim and stumbled upon Nelson—just an innocent dog romping playfully in the field." Su spoke matter-of-factly.

Jazzi was really worked up now. "We CAN'T just stand here!" she screamed. "We've got to do something *now* or Nelson's toast!"

Oxford was standing off to the side by himself. He was so overwhelmed by what he saw he couldn't think straight. His eyes were practically bugging out of his head and he was saying things that made no sense at all.

"Ohhh…," he groaned, "I bet that beast makes lovely hissing sounds as it hunts its prey, luring unassuming victims to go running into the fields to play but…," Oxford rambled on, "…they're never, ever seen again—not by their friends—not by their family—not by anyone. They're crushed—swallowed up—engulfed like a sweet gourmet treat." Beads of sweat trickled down his face as he frantically scrolled through his iNo.

Jazzi, realizing Oxford was having a melt-down, walked over, grabbed him by his shoulders and started shaking him. "Earth to Oxford! Earth to Oxford! If anyone's going to have a melt-down it should be me. You know what I've been through!" She continued to jerk him back and forth. "Don't make me have to slap you."

"He's in shock," Su said, poking Jazzi in the ribs. "Just give him a minute, he'll be fine."

"I'm sorry," she seethed, "poor timing! He needs to help me free Nelson from the grip of that evil serpent!"

Jazzi was growing angrier by the minute when two girls sauntered over, arm in arm, and introduced themselves.

"I'm Rachele," said the oldest girl. "This is my sister, Kristina. It appears your dog has met Pookie." She nodded toward the boa.

"What? Was there a choice?" Jazzi was taken aback. "I'm sorry but I don't have time to make friends right now, I need to get my dog back!"

"Don't worry," replied Rachele. "Pookie's big but he's harmless."

"He likes to play," Kristina explained.

"Play?" Jazzi put her hands on her hips and replied sternly, "Does my dog look like he's having a good time to you?"

Rachele looked up at Nafferton and said, "Have Pookie put the nice doggie down."

"Pip, pip—cheerio!" Nafferton gave three quick taps with his cane, and his oversized companion obediently lowered Nelson back to earth. The kids watched in awe as Nafferton twirled his monocle, let out a series of yips, then slid down on his stomach and landed in the crease of Pookie's neck. From there, he reached up with his cane and hooked onto a branch, then effortlessly pulled himself up like he was in a circus act. Swinging back and forth merrily, he acknowledged Rachele with an upturned lip and wink of an eye. She held out her skirt and curtsied to show her appreciation.

Jazzi watched speechless—she couldn't believe her eyes.

Once Nelson was back on all fours, he ran over and cowered behind her. Cat-Man-Doo sat beside him, licking his fur. She knew it could have just as easily been her swinging from the boa's merciless grip.

Rachele bent over to pet Nelson and then looked up at Jazzi. "Pookie's a rescue snake."

Jazzi rolled her eyes. "Who knew?"

"Ya, I found out when I was volunteering at the shelter. I heard they were having a difficult time finding him a home."

"Um—let's see—because of his humongous size?" Jazzi smirked, sarcastically. She stretched out her arms as far as they could reach, trying to make a point.

"That and his diet," Rachele replied with a compassionate heart. "Some people are squeamish."

Jazzi stared wide-eyed—she was *one* of the squeamish.

"You know it's really quite puzzling how he wound up here. Boa constrictors usually live in tropical areas."

"What's puzzling is why he decided to wind himself around my Nelson!" Jazzi said bitterly. "Didn't you ever consider rescuing something smaller, like maybe, a cat or dog or— horse?"

Rachele shook her head and sighed. "It was destiny."

Kristina stood rocking from side to side, hugging herself. "He's family."

"I didn't know you could get so attached to a snake." Jazzi said, backing away.

Oxford had finally snapped back to his old self and strolled over to join in conversation with the three girls. "Hey, I'm Oxy—what's up with the wiener dog?" No one replied. "Did I miss something?"

Jazzi looked at Oxford with a raised brow. "Miss something? Don't get me started, mister. This is Rachele and Kristina and they're in the middle of explaining Pookie and Nafferton." She turned back to the sisters. "Go on, girls."

"I was about to say that once we realized Pookie was visually challenged...," Rachele continued.

"He kept running into things." Kristina interrupted.

"That was a clue," Su said, forming a mental picture.

"Ya," Rachele nodded. "He nearly crushed Nafferton to pieces."

Jazzi's eyes widened. "How's that?"

"It was an accident. Nafferton was strolling through the flower fields, pushing a baby carriage, when he happened to cross Pookie's path. No one saw it coming." Kristina looked off into the distance.

"What happened to the baby?" Jazzi asked concerned.

"He was fine, but after that Nafferton figured he would live longer if he gave up his au pair job and volunteered to be Pookie's pilot instead."

"Sounds like a wise career move," Su agreed.

"Au pair?" Jazzi frowned.

Oxford had his iNo opened, prepared to give an answer.

"An au pair, Jazzi, is a foreigner who lives in someone's home and takes care of their children in exchange for room and board. Sort of like a nanny."

"Wasn't Nafferton afraid of Pookie after the incident?" Jazzi questioned Kristina.

"Nafferton felt it was in his best interest to forgive and move on," she replied.

Forgive? That's weird, Jazzi thought to herself.

"Excuse us," the girls said in unison. "We would like to be part of the Kids' Worldwide Peace Club. You're all over the blogs and we want to join you."

"But what about monster boy—er—I mean Pookie?" Oxford asked nervously.

"Oh, he's over the weight limit, we'll have to leave him at home."

"That's a relief." Oxford caught himself. "No, shame—I mean shame—its a *real* shame. Another time, perhaps? Bye-bye!" He turned and gave Pookie a fake little wave. *Hmmm,* he worried to himself, *somehow I don't think that's the end of Pookie and pal.*

Nafferton dipped the brim of his hat and bid a fond adieu to the kids. Pookie opened his mouth and, unfolding his long slinky tongue, waved fond farewells to all of his new friends.

Nelson stayed close to Jazzi, just to be on the safe side. He wasn't convinced Pookie was finished with his playtime. Hanging from a tree with a boa wrapped around your neck was not his idea of fun.

"Are you sure you want to join us?" Jazzi liked the idea of having female companionship, especially when English was their second language, but she was curious as to why they wanted to come. If you didn't count the oversized boa and its tiny talking wiener dog incident, Holland seemed quite serene.

Rachele looked at Jazzi and spoke frankly. "Even though people think of Holland as being rather open-minded, my sister and I live very sheltered lives. If we are to truly understand peace, it's only fair we explore different parts of the world."

"Then let your family know," Jazzi said, motioning to them. "Peace is a tricky thing, and we don't have much more time to figure it out."

The kids headed back toward the module, while the sisters ran off to say their goodbyes. It wasn't long before they were squeezing into the module and on their way to a new adventure. First-time visitors were especially fun to watch. The sensation of being shot up or down like a speeding bullet headed for its target, tended to make one's head spin.

While Haley was accommodating the new arrivals, Su was back in his seat replaying the whole Pookie and Nafferton scene in his head. It was mindboggling to say the least—he couldn't even imagine where Jazzi's mystery map would take them next."

CHAPTER 16

OJITOS BANDITOS

Mexico!" Jazzi shouted out, elated "The X is over La Paz, Mexico. Maybe it's Ojitos!"

"What's an Ojitos?" Oxford asked, scrolling through his iNo.

"Ojitos happens to be one of my most favorite friends on this entire planet. I'm sure he's been e-mailing you or we wouldn't be headed there."

"Geez, sorry, thought it was something to eat." Oxford searched through his messages. "Oh, yeah, here it is—heh heh—must have been an oversight."

"I met Ojitos when he was an exchange student, and he's *soooo* cute. I can hardly wait to see him." Jazzi cooed.

"*Ooohhh Ojitos, he's sooooo cute.*" Oxford tossed his head from side to side, mimicking Jazzi.

"I heard that!" she snapped.

Embarrassed, Oxford decided to refocus and send a Ojitos a text. Su punched in the keys to their new destination and off they went.

"Oooh . . ." Oxford whined, "this is the part my stomach hates!"

After a relatively smooth landing, the peace club walked down the familiar platform, excited to discover new names. There was Enrique, Selena, Poncho Villa, and a large colorful mural of a man with the word *Juan* written under it.

"Who's Juan?" Jazzi turned and faced Su.

"Graffiti artist?" he shrugged. "No one seems to know."

Hayley peered through the window and gave a friendly wave as the kids entered the module. Cat-Man-Doo trotted in bravely behind Nelson and curled up beside him. Together they shot up to the surface and leaped out onto the beautiful beach that looked out over the calm waters of Bahia de La Paz.

Oxford looked up from his iNo and stated, "It's interesting to note that the English translation of Bahia de La Paz is the Bay of Peace."

"That's perfect!" Jazzi jumped up and down. "This is it! I just know we'll find our answer here."

The water lapped gently along the sandy white beach and reflected the sunlight like hundreds of tiny mirrors. All along the beach they could see rows of cabanas, and on the boardwalk were little shops filled with brightly colored souvenirs. But their moment of serenity didn't last long when a thunderous roar began to reverberate through the air, shaking the ground beneath them.

"That's annoying." Jazzi cupped her hands over her ears.

Oxford turned and peered down the boardwalk. His face grew suddenly white. "Uh-oh…" he warned. "Banditos!"

"Banditos?" Jazzi repeated.

"Look!" Oxford pointed.

From out of nowhere, a gang of Mexican bandits sped toward the kids on their Harleys, blinding the young tourists in a whirling cloud of dust. They began circling around and around, shouting obscenities and making rude gestures. The kids huddled together, trying to get out of the banditos path, but it just made them angrier. Fear drenched the air like hot sauce on a tamale when an unshaven, gnarly tattooed dude hopped off his bike and pulled a pistol from his belt.

The kids' jumped back in shock. Was their search for peace about to end?

"Hand over your platinum cards," demanded the intimidating bandit.

Jazzi frowned. "Our what?"

"You heard me!" he said, scowling at her.

"Our platinum cards?" Jazzi repeated sarcastically. "You must be joking!"

"Do I look like I'm joking? I want all your loot and your plastic too!"

The kids started emptying their pockets, throwing what little contents they had onto the ground.

"WAIT!" Jazzi yelled, "Don't give that maniac another cent!" She turned and glared at the bandito. "This is CRAZY! You think we were sent here on a mission to fill *your* pockets?" She shook her head appalled. "And how do you expect us to turn over our platinum cards when we're not even old enough to have credit?"

At that moment Oxford began wheezing from all the dust. It started out slowly, but quickly advanced into a loud unsettling noise.

"SHUT UP, kid!" The gang leader grabbed Oxford by the throat and lifted him off the ground. "You're bothering me." Oxford's eyes grew as big as saucers as he struggled to breathe.

Jazzi leaped forward and screamed, "Leave him alone or I'll…I'll…!"

The outlaw burst out laughing. "You'll what?"

"I'm, I'm—I'm not sure," Jazzi stammered, fumbling for words. "But you WON'T like it!"

"Is that a threat?" asked the bandito, spitting a wad of chewing tobacco next to Jazzi's foot.

Sensing danger, Nelson let out a vicious growl and lunged toward the angry man. He sank his teeth deep into the man's arm, forcing him to release his grip on Oxford's throat.

"OUCH!" The bandito yelled, trying to pry Nelson off of him. "Get your mangy mutt off me!"

Nelson took one more lunge at the man. He gripped the front of his shirt between his sharp canine teeth and ripped it completely open. Much to everyone's surprise, a twelve-inch tattoo of a peace symbol swelled across his hairy brown chest. Nelson stood on all fours, barking at the derelict biker, and then slowly backed away.

Jazzi's mouth dropped open. "Uhhhh," she sucked air. "A *peace* symbol? You have a peace symbol tattooed on your chest?"

"So what's it to ya?" the biker snarled.

Jazzi shook her head, repulsed by the tattoo. "I know your type, you're nothing but a-a-a peace fraud!" Jazzi pointed her finger at the bandit as if she were holding her own pistol. "If you're smart, bubba, you'll get right back on your bike and head out of town. A man should know his limitations."

"This can't be good," Oxford fretted.

Su, Finn, 'Enery, and the sisters didn't move a muscle. They stood like statues in a cemetery, watching nervously as Jazzi confronted El Bandito—she wasn't about to back down.

"That chick has guts!" 'Enery whispered to Su.

"Yeah," Su answered quietly, "either that or she's seen too many Clint Eastwood movies."

"No one messes with me," the bandit growled, "especially some pint-size chick like you!"

Jazzi had pushed the man to his limit. He jumped back on his Harley, revved up the engine and headed straight for her.

The kids let out bloodcurdling cries and raced back in the direction of the module as fast as their legs would carry them—the bikers were right on their heels.

"Hurry!" Su shouted. "They're gaining on us!"

Finn and Su, along with Rachele and Kristina, were the first ones back to safety. 'Enery was amazingly speedy, taking full advantage of his crutch to propel himself forward. Oxford clung tightly onto Cat-Man-Doo as he turned and swerved, trying to outmaneuver their pursuers. Once everyone had reached the module, they threw themselves inside, secured the door and waited with bated breath for Jazzi and Nelson. Jazzi was lagging behind, frantically trying to dodge the bikers when she tripped on a rock and fell. The map went flying out of her pocket. Nelson immediately ran to her side and resumed his role as guard-dog—he wasn't about to let anyone harm her. She was only a few feet from the safety of the module, but was growing weaker by the minute.

"Somebody grab the girl before she gets away!" yelled the leader. One of the gang members threw down his Harley, with the motor still running, and lunged for Jazzi. Nelson was ready for action and, remembering the bandito's trick, started blazing around in circles, kicking up sand so he couldn't see.

"Ahhh!" the bandit cried out, wreathing in pain. He started rubbing his eyes but the more he rubbed, the worse it became and the worse it became, the more he rubbed. It finally became so bad he rolled over and hit his head on a rock, knocking himself unconscious.

"The map, Jazzi—get the MAP!" Oxford hollered.

"I'm trying, I'm trying!" Jazzi lay helplessly sprawled out in the sand—she could see the map lying in front of her. She strained with all her might to touch it with her fingertips, but just as she was about to snag it, a gust of wind whisked it away—hopes of ever seeing it again were crushed.

"Oh no—now what am I to do?" She buried her head beneath her arms, overcome by exhaustion."

"Forget it, Jazzi!" Oxford stuck his arm outside the module door. "Try to grab my hand!"

"I can't, Oxy—I just can't..."

Jazzi peeked up at the module thinking it would be the last time she'd ever see her companions again and then—something caught her eye. She blinked a few times to make sure she wasn't hallucinating. Standing beside the module was a shadowy figure of a man with outstretched arms.

"*Are you an angel?* She looked into his face. "*Is it my time?*"

"Let me help you," he said with a calm smile. Jazzi stared into his kind blue eyes as he scooped her up into his arms and lifted her safely inside the module. When the module door closed, he was nowhere to be found.

Jazzi lay speechless on the floor looking up into the welcoming faces of her friends.

"You did it, Jazzi!" The kids gave a round of applause.

"How did I get here, Oxy?" she mumbled weakly.

He looked around hoping someone else would answer. "Hate to admit it, Jazzi, but I don't know. We were so busy trying to figure out how to save you that no one saw you slip in. Beats me how you managed to float inside without anyone noticing. Been practicing your magic?" He said jokingly, hoping to get her to smile."

"Are you positive?" Jazzi started to tear up. "None of you saw anyone lift me inside?"

"No…" Everyone shook their heads agreeing.

Oxford looked at her puzzled. "Someone lifted you?"

"Relax Jazzi, you've been through a lot." Su helped her to her feet.

"Hey, where's Nelson?" Jazzi started to panic. "And the map, where's the MAP?" She bolted to the door to see if she could spot Nelson, but instead, found herself face to face with the unsavory bandito who tried to grab her—his eyes were still red and irritated from the sand. But far worse, they were full of anger—dark and distant—void of any peace. He threw up his fist at her, blurted out a few curse words, then jumped back on his bike and trailed off into the distance.

"I hope that's the last we see of him and his sleazy sidekicks," Jazzi said, grabbing Su's arm. "Open the door, I have to find Nelson!"

"Slow down," he demanded. "You're not going out there alone."

Su pushed the button and the module door opened. "Stay in a group in case the banditos happen to show up," he ordered.

"Okay, okay," Jazzi agreed, "just go!"

As instructed, the kids didn't venture far from each other. They searched high and low, looking everywhere they could think of. The beach was vast and barren which meant the map could have landed anywhere.

Jazzi buried her face in her hands, she was furious with herself. How could she have left Nelson and the map behind?

"My poor Nelson, I hope someone finds him and gives him a good home."

"Stop worrying, Jazzi. I'm sure he's fine," said Finn.

"Well, *I'm* not fine and *none* of us will be if I don't find the map!" she growled. "We're lost without it."

"Listen to Finn, Jazzi. It doesn't do any good to get mad. What matters is that we're together," said Rachele. Kristina looked over at her sister and, together, they walked over to Jazzi and wrapped their arms around her.

Jazzi was so caught off guard by their display of affection, she didn't notice Nelson when he came prancing out from behind a pile of driftwood and laid something at her feet.

Oxford immediately bent over and picked it up. "Nice…!" He gave Nelson a quick pat on the head and tapped Jazzi on the shoulder. "Sorry to interrupt your little hug fest but…," Rachele and Kristina stepped back, "look who found the MAP!"

"Nelson? MAP?" Jazzi was elated—she knelt down and wrapped her arms around Nelson's neck. "I'm so happy to see you, boy—you saved the day!" The kids surrounded Jazzi and Nelson, hooting and hollering—feeling hopeful once again.

"See, Jazzi?" Finn beamed. "All things work together when you believe."

"Yup," 'Enery agreed. "I'm a believer!"

"I'm impressed you had the courage to stand up to that—that—pond scum!" Oxford hailed Jazzi in between an occasional wheeze. "You were totally brave!"

"Or completely psycho," Su laughed.

Jazzi lifted her finger as if she were holding a gun, pretending to blow off the rising smoke. "A girl's gotta do what a girl's gotta do!"

With her confidence restored, she brushed the sand off her clothes and straightened her hair. Then, taking a long deep breath, she gave a quick nod.

"Okay—shall we try this again?" She tucked the map deep inside her pocket, she wasn't about to risk losing it again.

The kids were still nervous as they headed back to the beach to find Ojitos. Those banditos were scary dudes! Jazzi found herself still looking around for the man who had saved her from an untimely death—there was no way she imagined him.

Once they arrived, smiles lit up their faces. It felt good knowing the banditos were really gone. Jazzi gazed out across the sand until she spotted a sign.

"Can you read that, Oxy?"

He adjusted his glasses for better focus. "It says 'Buenos Tamales' (ba-way-noes ta-mal-ees)."

"That's it! *Good Tamales*—that's the name of Nina's restaurant."

"So forgive my ignorance, Jazzi, but—Nina? Is that a side-dish to go with an order of Ojitos?" Oxford grabbed his stomach and bent over laughing.

Jazzi glared back with daggers in her eyes. "You're not funny! Guess I forgot to mention Nina is *la abuela* to Ojitos and his sister Raquel."

"*La abuela*? Grandmother? I'm impressed, didn't know you knew Spanish. I can put my iNo away now."

"Not so fast, Ojitos only taught me a few words," Jazzi said, still bent out of shape.

"Oh, Ojitos," Oxford sulked. "Of course."

Everyone was excited to see Ojitos—except for Oxford, that is—but that didn't stop him from joining the group as they flew down the beach like a flock of sandpipers.

Before long they stumbled upon a small outdoor café, located just outside town. It was a quaint little place—adobe pots overflowing with colorful succulents lined the walkway. Hanging above the entrance was a sign that read, "Buenos Tamales". Jazzi opened the door and peeked inside. Seeing a familiar face, she shouted, "Nina—NINA—it's me, JAZZI!"

"Jazzi?" replied a voice with a heavy Spanish accent. "*Ay Dios mio!*"

"What did she say?" Kristina nudged Oxford.

He grabbed his iNo. "She said, 'Oh my Lord!' It's an expression of joy."

Seconds later an older Mexican woman wearing a tamale-stained apron rushed to the door and grabbed Jazzi. She wrapped her up in her arms and squeezed her tightly to her chest. Jazzi smiled contentedly—it had been a long time since she had felt so much love.

"I'm so happy to see you, Nina and I can't wait to see Ojitos. It has been so long! Is he ready? We don't have much time."

"*Sí*, Ojitos is in the back room helping Raquel on the *computadora*."

Ojitos heard the commotion and came running out waving Oxford's downloaded message in his hand. He was quite handsome with a shock of jet-black hair and bright hazel eyes.

"Jazzi!" Ojitos smiled. "I can't believe you're finally here, and you've brought so many amigos."

Everyone waved and smiled back at him. Oxford stood off by himself, strangely quiet.

Jazzi threw her arms around Ojitos and planted a big kiss on his cheek—he blushed from ear to ear.

Oxford shifted uncomfortably from one foot to the other as a wave of jealousy surged up his spine.

"Wait until you see the CyberCoaster, Ojitos," Jazzi gushed. "We have so much to talk about. Is Raquel coming too?"

"She needs to stay and help Nina run the restaurant. Next time, perhaps."

"Ummm, those tamales smell great," 'Enery hinted.

"Where are my manners?" said Nina. "Raquel, fix a tray for our guests to take with them, *por favor*."

Raquel popped her head out of the back of the restaurant and smiled. "*Sí*, but be very careful when you eat them," she teased, "these tamales are chili today, but hot tamale."

"*Chicas*," Ojitos rolled his eyes and picked up his backpack. "C'mon, I'll lead the way."

"Adios!" the kids called out as they passed by Raquel and grabbed the tamales.

"*Vaya con Dios*," Nina and Raquel answered and waved back fondly. "Please be careful *mi niños*. It's a dangerous place we live in." Nina put her arm around Raquel and pulled her close.

"Don't worry," Jazzi reassured her. She scooted quickly past Nina and Raquel, hoping no one would bring up the bandito incident. Some things were just better left unsaid.

CHAPTER 17

HOT TAMALES!

Yum, warm tamales," Oxford said. He was looking forward to something other than a cyber-snack.

In fact, the anticipation of diving into one of Nina's tamales had everyone excited. It was just what they needed to move past the bandito nightmare and focus on their mission. Inside the CyberCoaster everybody eagerly awaited Hayley's assistance in preparing for takeoff. Su was in the process of taking another bite of tamale when he noticed his seatbelt wasn't secured. As he reached down to tighten it, the tamale dropped from his hand and spilled onto the mainframe's keyboard, soaking the entire system. Hoping his clumsy act would go unnoticed, he picked up a rag and started cleaning. Nelson sniffed the scent of food and rushed over to assist by lapping up all the juice his tongue could reach. Unfortunately, he licked something he shouldn't have, causing the power switches to activate all at once. The coaster automatically accelerated, blasting off with an unprepared pilot and a dog sliding down the aisle on all fours.

"Brace yourselves!" Su yelled as he fumbled about the keyboard, trying to gain control. He wasn't about to let anyone know what really happened.

"Ow," Oxford said, biting his tongue instead of the tamale, "that was unexpected."

"Is it always this jerky?" asked Ojitos, gripping his seat.

"No," replied Finn, "this is unusual." He held his tamale in one hand and adjusted his wedgie with the other.

Other kids joined in, voicing their concern—Su didn't say a word.

Before long Hayley stepped up to the front of the cabin and made an announcement. "We seem to be experiencing some unusual turbulence. Please keep your seatbelts fastened until I inform you otherwise."

Once Su managed to level off the coaster and gain back some control, he felt confident no one saw the tamale accident. "Where to now, Jazzi?" he shouted, as if nothing had happened.

"I'll try to look now that I'm not bouncing all over my seat." She wiped a dot of tamale juice off her arm.

Before Jazzi had a chance to open her mouth, Oxford blurted, "Hey, I just got an urgent e-mail from Jamaica."

"Maybe that's why the X is on Jamaica, mon!" Jazzi lit up. "Coincidence, Oxy?" She winked.

"Yup, the X just *happens* to be on Jamaica." Oxford rolled his eyes. "Apparently some kid from Kingston wants to meet up with us in Montego Bay. He and his reggae band are jammin' on the beach near a place called Dead Man's Cove."

In the background you could hear kids chanting, "Jamaica, mon—Jamaica, mon—we all be goin' to Jamaica, mon!"

Su gave a verbal command, directing the coaster to head toward Jamaica, but it seemed sluggish. There were obvious mechanical issues but he hoped in time they would iron themselves out. Jazzi was busy setting up her iPod and trying to persuade everyone to get up and dance. It didn't take much coaxing once she cranked up the music—kids were up and out of their seats in no time, swaying back and forth to the rhythm. Oxford chose to sit back and sulk—he found no pleasure in watching Ojitos show off his dance moves with Jazzi.

From the corner of her eye, Jazzi noticed Oxford staring at her and started clapping and shouting. "C'mon everyone, give it up for Oxford! Go Oxy—Go Oxy—Go Oxy!"

Oxford was truly feeling the pressure and had no choice but to stand up and move to the cheering crowd, but—he was definitely not in sync. Whichever way the kids moved, he seemed to be moving in the opposite direction.

"Oh, Oxy, when it comes to dancing, you're such a moron," Jazzi teased, "a real *oxymoron!*" She giggled and slapped him on the back. "Get it?"

"Surprised *you* know what that means," he retaliated.

"Geez," Jazzi said, "looks like somebody woke up on the wrong side of the world today."

"You're a real comedian," Oxford grumbled to himself. Feeling a bit perturbed, he decided to sit down and e-mail a reply back to Montego Bay announcing their ETA.

Su continued to wipe up the keyboard while everyone was distracted. He was hoping he hadn't damaged any internal components. It was still sticky with tamale residue and wasn't reacting the way it should. He tried typing in different coordinates but nothing changed. The CyberCoaster simply wasn't performing up to par and he was getting concerned. He tried pushing another button but that made things worse. The coaster began to quiver and shake, followed by an upward jerk, then sudden downward spiral. The kids clung to each other to keep from falling when—much to their surprise…

"*Ay caramba,*" moaned Ojitos as he looked up through the glass ceiling. "You mean we have to swim to get out?"

"Oops!" Su gazed out the window in shock. "Everyone be calm." He broke into a serious sweat. "Heh, heh—must have pushed a wrong button. Yup, sorry 'bout that, but the good news is—we're in Jamaica!"

It was obvious the coaster had strayed off course, and they were now submerged under miles of clear blue sea. The tamale sauce spill was more serious than Su had previously thought. He felt terrible knowing it was his fault, but when the cyber-doors jutted open and water started pouring in—he was devastated! Shouts and screams filled the air as streams of water quickly turned into peaking waves that were certain to flood the entire cabin. The only way out was to swim!

"Keep your heads up!" Oxford yelled.

"Stand on your seat!" Finn screamed.

Su attacked the keyboard, frantically trying to close the doors, but the water continued surging in. Higher and higher it rose; first to their knees, then their waists, and before long they were up to their necks in salt water.

Jazzi was terrified. "Hurry, Su!" She let out a bloodcurdling shriek and pointed to the door. "Oh No—the map—the MAP!"

Oxford stared in horror as their most valued possession floated toward the open door. 'Enery struggled to stop it with his crutch, but the current was too strong. Ojitos swam over to grab it, but just as his fingers touched it, Jazzi fell off her seat and distracted him. Down she went, completely submerged underwater.

"Jazzi!" Ojitos cried out. He plugged his nose and started to dive down after her when, all at once, she surfaced, sputtering and coughing up water.

"You alright?" Oxford yelled over the rushing water.

She pushed her wet locks aside and cried out, "No, I'm *not* alright—we're doomed without the map!"

"There's nothing you can do about it now. Let it go, Jazzi!" Oxford said, spitting water with every word.

"Oh yeah, well it's gonna take more than a little water to stop me. I'm goin' back down."

"Don't do it, Jazzi!" Ojitos pleaded, but it was too late.

Jazzi dove off the seat, but before she was able to take a stroke, Nelson jumped in behind her and bit down on the seat of her pants. Slowly he turned her around and paddled back to her seat.

"Stop it, Nelson, let go of me!" Jazzi scolded and fought him the entire time, but he wasn't about to release her.

"It's okay, Jazzi," Ojitos tried to reason with her. "Nelson doesn't want you to get hurt either and, once Su has fixed the problem, we can all help look for the map."

"You don't understand," said Jazzi, panicked. "We need to find it before it floats out to sea!"

"We will, we will," Oxford assured her. "Su is working on it now."

Su was now underwater, holding his breath, hacking away at the keyboard. It was imperative that he stop the water from flowing in or they would surely drown. With the final slam of the 'enter' key, the doors slammed shut. They were up to their necks in water, but fortunately, there was a pocket of air inside the cabin so they could breathe.

The inside of the CyberCoaster was quite a sight: swimming kids, drifting animals, soggy tamales—it was a mess. Hayley floated through the cabin wearing swim fins, goggles, and an inflatable rubber duck. Su stood on his seat and reported that he was proud to have made some headway—the salt-water had been a big help. Of course he forgot to mention that it helped by washing away the rest of the sticky tamale juice. Feeling a bit full of himself, he decided to try one more thing. He held his nose, jumped back in and swam down to the floor of the coaster. He was hoping to find the switch that would redirect the coaster back to its original destination, but whatever he pushed sent the CyberCoaster reeling back and forth with such intensity, waves started to form inside the cabin.

"Uh Oh—Surf's up?" Ojitos lifted himself up onto an overhead compartment to keep from being hit by an oncoming wave.

"Ohhh…," Oxford moaned. "Now I'm seasick."

The kids hung on to anything they could grab hold of to keep from sinking—it was like riding inside a giant tidal wave. But, miraculously, Su was able to release the exit doors, and with a mighty rush, tons of water started pouring out, taking everyone right along with it. Haley had lodged the rubber duck between two seats to keep from floating away and yelled, "Don't give up!" as kids and animals were swept out the door. The force of the water pushed them down to the bottom of the ocean and into a hole that led back inside the tunnels. It felt like they were on a waterpark slide, being sucked down inside a long winding tube. Splats of water followed by a thud and several moans made it obvious that it was a hard landing.

Ojitos sat up on the platform, surprised. "Wow, how did we get here? Last thing I remember was being pulled under water. It felt strange, like I was swirling inside a suction cup"

"Allow me to explain," said Su, his mind racing. He actually had no idea how they had ended up back on the platform, so he quickly made something up.

"You see, the CyberCoaster stirred up a whirlwind of water which, in turn, created a funnel or, as scientists prefer to call it—a vortex. We were literally sucked inside the vortex and forced down through an opening in the bottom of the sea which eventually led us here—back to the exact spot we were destined to be." He was pretty pleased with his performance and hoped everyone had bought into it. He was a bit nervous Oxford might search his iNo, however.

Oxford wiped the water from his glasses. "But that's nearly impossible, Su. I don't believe scientists have ever found an opening in the floor of the ocean."

Jazzi stuck her face up to Oxfords and shouted. "Who cares what you think? A lot of things don't make sense but we're here—we're safe—and that's ALL that matters!"

"Are we Jazzi—are we *really* safe?" Oxford wasn't buying any of Su's scientific mumbo jumbo, but it was easier than going head to head with Jazzi. Right or wrong she always managed to come out on top—he never understood that.

"What about Hayley and the CyberCoaster, Su? Are they still floating around up there?" Finn asked, curious.

Su crossed his fingers behind his back. "Of course, just like I planned."

Whether or not anyone believed Su's theory, they were happy to be alive and on dry ground. Nelson stood near Jazzi shaking water off his back and flinging it on to everyone else. Cat-Man-Doo politely licked her fur so she wouldn't look like a drowned rat. Though soggy and out of breath, no one complained—they stared up at the ceiling, waiting to see what would come next.

Ojitos took it upon himself to read aloud the sayings that were written on the wall.

"*De be no truth but de One truth*, signed Bob Marley." His eyes moved feverishly across the wall. "Hey, listen to this one, *De owly ting we av to dread iz dreads dey self.* I bet this one was written by Bob Marley's barber," he chuckled.

"Who's Bob Marley, Oxy?" Jazzi asked, twisting her curls to wring the water out.

Oxford dried his iNo screen and began his usual rant. "Bob Marley was a famous Jamaican balladeer and philosopher who…"

"I don't need all the details," Jazzi cut in, "but what's a balladeer?"

"A balladeer is a singer," Oxford snapped. "Okay?" He turned and looked away.

"Fine," Jazzi replied angrily. "You don't have to act so grumpy just because the map is gone. So I lost the key to our whole mission—get over it!"

I guess I should just calmly accept it, huh, Jazzi? Wait, what were those words that had you so concerned again? Ummm, oh yeah, I think it was something like, 'No matter what—DON'T LOSE THE MAP'!"

"Whatever." Jazzi rolled her eyes. "I'll figure it out."

Her words were soon interrupted by the sound of the module door sliding open. The kids picked themselves up and stepped aboard, wet clothes and all. A tropical blue light filtered through the glass top as the module broke through to the surface, revealing a spectacular island paradise. Doors clanged open to glistening rays of sunlight dancing on the sand. Jazzi stepped out first, leaving a trail of water behind her. She took a few steps then stopped and closed her eyes. She could feel the hot sun beating down on her skin through her wet clothes. "Ahhh...this feels good." She took a deep breath and lifted her head towards the sky. "I could stand here all day."

"Yes, I know, but we're on a mission—remember?" Su tugged at Jazzi's arm.

"Alright...alright, but the map is gone and it's all my fault!" Jazzi stared down at the ground moping.

"Don't beat yourself up, Jazzi." said Su. "We're all in this together—we'll make it work."

"Yeah." Oxford shuffled his feet. "Sorry I yelled."

"Thanks," Jazzi replied, "but where do we go from here?"

Oxford pulled out a piece of paper. "My wet e-mail says to go..."

"Forget your soggy e-mail," Ojitos jumped in. "Listen to the music and follow your ears." He raised his arms and swayed his hips to the rhythm of the tropical beat. "Follow me!"

CHAPTER 18

THE COLOR OF SHADOWS

G reat idea, Ojitos!" Jazzi's spirit lifted.

"Yeah, swell," muttered Oxford, feeling pangs of jealousy. "Who needs a map when you have Ojitos—I mean music?" He bobbed his head around, trying to imitate Ojitos with a whiney voice. He wasn't a big fan.

"C'mon," Ojitos hollered, motioning to the kids. He tuned in to the rhythm of the pounding reggae music and let his ears be their guide. Nelson and Cat-Man-Doo sashayed behind, prancing to the melody as if they had rehearsed in advance. It wasn't long before they stumbled upon a group of musicians, surrounded by a crowd of cheering spectators, dancing and clapping. Since Jazzi felt responsible for losing the map, she jerked the e-mail from Oxford's hand and danced her way to the front of the crowd.

"Hey guys—over here!" She waved the soggy paper in the air to get the band's attention.

107

The bandleader noticed her right away and called out, "Be wid yu inna minud, mon!"

Jazzi turned to Oxford. "What kind of language is that?" She was hoping he was in a better mood now that they were standing together with their group.

"It's called Rasta…Ra-sta; Patois….pat-wa, but the Jamaicans call it *real* English." Oxford read confidently from his iNo, although his sulky attitude was still noticeable.

After the jam session ended, the band members began packing up their instruments and other belongings. The dreadlocked leader sidestepped over to introduce himself to Jazzi and friends. His dark matted hair fell handsomely below his shoulders. He and Da Boyz all wore brightly colored Caribbean shirts with baggy shorts and sandals.

"Me be Jammin' Jamal an dis be me band, me bruddahs—Da Boyz."

Jazzi struggled to understand his heavy accent.

Jamal and Da Boyz were from Kingston, located on the other side of the island from Montego Bay. They had very dark skin, almost black. Their teeth shone a brilliant white by comparison, like piano keys smiling across a grand piano.

Oxford had once explained his theory of skin color to Jazzi: "Whiteness or darkness is merely the result of reflected light. It's a scientific fact that white skin reflects more light than dark skin and dark skin absorbs more light, creating the illusion of darkness. It's all just simple physics. If there were no light at all," he had said, "we would all be the same color—the color of shadows."

"Remember what you told me about skin color?" Jazzi said.

Oxford nodded.

"If that's true then technically we're all the same color when the lights go out, right?"

"Guess you could say that," Oxford replied.

"Then why can I see my freckles in the dark?"

Oxford walked off shaking his head. Jazzi loved to push his buttons—he learned it was less stressful to ignore her at times.

Jazzi turned to Jamal and Da Boyz. "Which one of you is the representative?"

"We all be!" Jamal beamed.

"All of you?" She stepped back, surprised.

"Dat be right. Kingston be a veree dangerous place, like da war zone. Me and Da Boyz want to stop de fighting, make it a safer place. We be a team dat sticks together."

The band, along with their guitars, horns, keyboard, and drums, started to head toward the module when they were suddenly startled by a cry for help.

"Sounds like someone's in trouble!" yelled 'Enery.

Jamal shouted. "Let's go, mon!"

The band laid their gear back down and followed behind the kids as Jamal led them down the beach a short distance to a spot called Dead Man's Cove. He came to an abrupt halt when there, lying in the sand, were Oxford's rumpled up clothes and his black-framed glasses.

"Over here!" Rachele yelled. "I found Oxford's iNo!"

"*What?* He never goes anywhere without his iNo!" Jazzi leaned over, speechless. "How can this be? He was just with us!"

"I saw him wander off while you were talking to Jamal," said Finn. "I just figured he needed some space. He seemed kind of edgy."

"Space? Edgy?" Jazzi yelled. "We don't have time for that!"

She turned to Nelson and commanded, "Go find Oxy, boy!"

Nelson took off with Cat-Man-Doo trailing behind. Together they combed the sandy white beach, sniffing every inch, looking for signs of life.

Meanwhile the other kids, along with Jamal and Da Boyz, spread out in all directions, searching for clues.

"Hey—I found him!" shouted Ojitos.

Jazzi was the first to arrive—the others were quick to join her. Entangled in a large clump of seaweed beneath a swarm of squawky seagulls, Oxford lay gasping for air.

A dark shadow of a man loomed over him.

Jazzi stared up at the figure, shocked to see a familiar face. "Sir Sean," she rubbed her eyes, "is…is that you?"

The tall-framed character stood silently smiling down at her.

"What have you done to Oxy?" she demanded.

Oxford shook his head weakly. The gel from his wet hair acted like cement, causing sand and seaweed to stick like glue to his unruly red locks.

"No, NO, he didn't do anything, Jazzi—except save my life," he choked. "I was in a bad mood and decided to go for a swim and then…"

"What?" Jazzi howled. "That's why your things were lying in the sand and you were nowhere to be found? Because you were in a *bad mood* and decided to go for a swim?"

She was getting worked up now.

"Didn't we just finish swimming inside the CyberCoaster? How could you be so insensitive? I thought something awful had happened!" Jazzi buried her face in her hands and began to cry.

Oxford stared speechless, surprised by Jazzi's outburst. Feeling awkward, he looked up at Jamal for support. "That didn't go well," he said, grinning sheepishly.

Jamal rolled his eyes at Oxford and began singing a Bob Marley song, "No Woman, No Cry." The words fit the occasion—he knew Oxford's pain had just begun.

"Wen a mon cares dat mush bout a wo-mon an she knos it," he said, "well der be no lettin' up on him fer a long time."

As far as Jamal was concerned, Oxford would hear about this for possibly the rest of his life. He took a step back and rubbed his chin, examining Oxford up and down.

"You be pretty brave, Ox' mon. Me an Da Boyz won't go in da water. Dey call dis Dead Mon's Cave for a reezon!" He reached in his bag and handed Oxford an official pair of Slam Jammin' Jamal's island shorts. "Here, put deez on." He helped Oxford to his feet and handed him a towel so he could slip into his new board shorts. "You gonna be stylin' wi da brudahs now."

"Gee, thanks guys!" Oxford grinned as he pulled a piece of seaweed off his lip.

"Are you kidding?" Jazzi threw her hands up and collapsed onto the sand. "I hardly think a reward is necessary. He practically ruined the entire day by disrupting our plans, making us worry and…and…all the other stuff!"

"Now don't fret, lass," Sir Sean knelt down beside her, "he's part of your mission, you need him."

"I don't need him or anyone else!" She scolded Sir Sean. "And you? I thought you had disappeared in the clouds never to be seen again!"

He smiled at her with his kind blue eyes.

"Ah," the pirate said with a wink, "ye never know fer sure where I might turn up. But as luck would 'ave it I just happened to be nearby fer your friend here. Guess he underestimated the current."

Rachele and Kristina saw Jazzi was upset, but they were much more interested in watching Oxford strut around in his new board shorts.

Sir Sean stood up and patted Jazzi on the shoulder, but she promptly brushed his hand away—he didn't take it personally. He turned around to Oxford and gave him a thumbs-up— he was still caught up in the moment, modeling his new look. Meanwhile, Jazzi was becoming more and more irritated. Not one person had even noticed her pouty face— she felt completely ignored. Who would have thought that finding Oxford would turn into a celebration? It was his fault for wandering away! To make matters worse, he was parading around trying to make a fashion statement without *her* approval!

Despite Jazzi's poor attitude, Sir Sean tapped her on the shoulder and slipped a rolled-up piece of parchment paper into her hand. "Don't ferget this, lass, ye may need it."

Jazzi begrudgingly unrolled the paper, frowning "What's this? A map? Wait—*the* MAP? Impossible! How did you get it? I thought it was forever lost at sea. I thought we'd never be able to complete our mission."

When the others heard the good news, they all came running over.

She looked over at her friends, then down at the ground and back up at Sir Sean. "Sorry," she whimpered with puppy dog eyes.

The group waited anxiously, wondering what would come out of her mouth next.

Jazzi kicked at the sand, hemming and hawing, trying to come up with the right words. "Well—I—um," she stammered, "What I'm trying to say is THANK YOU! Now we can finish what we started!" She jumped up and gave him a big hug.

Sir Sean blushed and backed away, tipping his hat. He bowed politely to Jazzi and the others, then excused himself and disappeared inside a cloud of birds.

"Wow—how does he do that?" Jazzi shook her head and gave Oxford a slight grin. Nelson and Cat-Man-Doo were huddled together off to the side, disappointed their cleverly plotted bird chase scheme had foiled.

Now that Jazzi was her old self again, the kids felt it was safe to be near her and gathered around to view the map. "This is where we are right now," she pointed to a small red X, "and this X..."

Ojitos jumped in, "Marks a new adventure! C'mon, let's get outta here. I'm hot and sticky."

"One small detail," said Oxford.

All eyes were on him, waiting to hear what he was about to say.

"The CyberCoaster—it will be difficult to leave if we can't find it."

"Oxy, Oxy, when are you going to learn to trust me?" Su shook his head. "Follow me..."

CHAPTER 19

FROZEN WITH FEAR

Jazzi glanced up at the darkening sky. "We'd better listen to Su if we have any hopes of getting out of here."

Jamal and Da Boyz packed up their gear and followed Su and the other kids to the spot where the module would have brought them, had they not gone off track. Su climbed up on a rock wall and looked out over the water.

"Over there!" he pointed. "Right there in plain view." Secretly he was shocked that he had spotted it so easily. He could always count on Hayley.

"Now, all we have to do is get to it," said 'Enery.

"I'm really not in the mood to swim, Su, so what do you suggest?" Jazzi whined.

Ojitos jumped up on the wall beside Su. "Hey, there's a fishing boat on the other side of the wall. Maybe I can find the owner and ask them for help," he suggested.

As much as Oxford didn't want to admit it, he thought Ojitos' plan was smart and offered to go with him to try and find the owner. As they neared the boat they noticed an old fisherman sitting beside it cleaning his fish.

"Nice catch!" Oxford grinned.

"Thanks," replied the old man, his weathered face was partially hidden beneath the floppy brim of his hat. "What can I do fer ya?"

"We were wondering if you might be able to help us," Ojitos asked politely.

He peered up from under his hat. "How's that?"

Oxford stepped closer. "My friends and I were hoping you could give us a ride to our...our...," he paused, unsure of what to say, "...our boat? It's over there."

The old fisherman laughed. "I was wonderin' who that big ole contraption belonged to. Looks like one of them there alien ships—know what I mean?"

The boys nodded their heads, pretending to agree.

"How many of ya are there?"

Ojitos starting counting out loud in Spanish.

"What'd he say?"

"He said it will probably take two trips." replied Oxford. "We'll gladly pay you."

"Nah," he answered, "I don't want yer money, but hurry along before it's too dark to see."

With that, Oxford and Ojitos ran back to round up the group.

"Everyone grab your stuff, we found a ride," Ojitos said, excited.

"But we'll have to make two trips, so split up," Oxford added.

After it was decided who was to go first, the kids rushed over to the boat and introduced themselves. The fisherman gave a welcoming nod and helped the first group step inside the boat. Su wanted to be first to board, just in case there were any surprises. He picked up Cat-Man-Doo and tucked her under his arm then hopped in. Jazzi and Nelson were next, followed by Rachele, Kristina and 'Enery. Upon arrival, Su was quite relieved to see that Hayley had everything cleaned up and ready to go. Once everyone had boarded, the fisherman turned his boat around and headed back to get the second batch of kids. Oxford had waited behind so he could help Ojitos load up Jamal and Da Boyz'. It wasn't going to be easy to cram all their instruments in.

On the way back to the CyberCoaster, the old man took a drag on his pipe and leaned over to Oxford—his breath smelled like musty old tobacco. "That's some rig you got there. Never seen anything like it in all my years of fishin'."

"Yup, it's unique, alright." Oxford held his breath and pulled away. He preferred to leave it at that.

The kid's thanked the man for being so kind and watched as he motored out of sight.

Hayley welcomed the new passengers and helped them settle in. One of Da Boyz wasn't paying any attention and continued to hold his travel bag on his lap.

"Put that bag under the seat in front of you," Haley instructed.

"Wot?"

"Please put your bag in that empty spot under the seat in front of you."

"Wot?" he repeated, still confused.

"Ey mom—I sed pud de bag unda de seat!"

Everybody put whatever they had under the seat and said no more.

"Tank ju berry mush." Hayley nodded then continued on with business.

Jazzi plopped down next to Oxford and began scanning the map for their next destination. He closed his eyes, hoping to blend into the seat and avoid another lecture. It had finally dawned on him that sneaking off to the beach for a little cave time probably wasn't such a good idea.

"Oxy," Jazzi poked him, "how did Sir Sean get the map when it was last seen floating out to sea?" Oxford grunted, pretending to be asleep, so Jazzi moved across the aisle next to Ojitos. He had been listening to every word, trying to figure out who Sir Sean was.

"Look, Ojitos," said Jazzi, spreading the map over his lap, "the X is over Alaska." She took a second look. "Girdwood, Alaska?" She wrapped her arms around herself and pretended she was shivering. "Brrrrrr . . ."

"*Sí*," Ojitos agreed. "Will Sir Sean be there?"

Jazzi looked at him peculiarly. "I have no idea."

Su punched in the appropriate keys to make the coaster airtight like a submarine. That would allow them to submerge underwater and travel back down into the tunnels where they needed to be. Once they were back on track, they could continue on to Alaska.

The jolt from takeoff shot Oxford straight up in his seat, startling him. "Whoa," he huffed. "Sorry, I must have fallen asleep. Where are we headed, Jazzi?"

"The last place I would have picked," she grumbled. "Girdwood, Alaska. Who goes there?"

"Apparently, we are." Oxford searched his iNo and confidently reported, "Did you know that Girdwood, Alaska was originally named Glacier City and while it began as a supply camp for gold miners at the turn of the century, it's now considered Alaska's only true resort town?"

"Thank you for that important news flash, Oxy. I'm sure we'll all sleep sounder." Jazzi sank back in her seat and pulled a blanket up around her neck, but before her eyes closed, 'Enery's shouts signaled they had already arrived.

"Check it out!" 'Enery hollered. "Did ya know there are giant icicles in Alaska and ther danglin' above our 'eads?"

The passengers immediately stopped what they were doing and looked up.

"Su, you cheeky devil, it's just an optical illusion to trick us—right? 'Enery grabbed his belly laughing.

Finn's eyes widened. "Wow, they look razor-sharp! Don't think they're fake 'Enery."

"You're right, Finn," Su gulped. "It's no illusion!"

Instead of the usual multicolored rock shards and diamond-encrusted teeth, hundreds of lethal ice needles hung perilously overhead the coaster.

Ojitos gazed up through the glass roof. "We're sittin' ducks! One false move and those icicles become weapons of mass destruction."

"Su!" Jazzi threw off her blanket and climbed up on her knees. "Now what's happening?" She held onto the back of her seat to keep from falling.

"Not sure, just hang on!" he called back.

"We could be in serious trouble if there were an earthquake," Oxford said, worried.

Unexpectedly, the CyberCoaster jolted, knocking Jazzi back into her seat.

Hayley moved to the front of the cabin, holding onto the seats for support. "Please remain seated as we are experiencing some unexpected turbulence."

"Gee, where have I heard those words before?" Jazzi grumbled.

"Keep your seatbelts securely fastened until otherwise noted." Hayley gave Jazzi a stern look.

Unfamiliar with this type of incident, Su accidently set off the emergency alarm. A shrill ear-piercing siren reverberated throughout the coaster.

"AHHHHH!" everyone grabbed their ears.

"Don't worry, I've got it!" Su said, raising his voice above the shouts. He was quick to disable the alarm, but was completely caught off guard when the CyberCoaster began to slide. Crackling sounds erupted like fireworks as it bumped up against frozen tunnel walls, causing the deadly icicles to split in half. Su tried desperately to steer the coaster, dodging and swerving, barely missing the ice shards as they came crashing down around them.

"I think something is interfering with the magnets!" Su yelled, struggling to maintain control.

"What are magnets, Su?" Kristina asked, concerned.

Su shouted back, "Magnets have the power to attract other magnetic material such as iron. Simply stated they are what keep the coaster hovering over the track. The problem is they seem to be freezing over which is disturbing the connection."

"Freezing over?" Oxford's voice shook as everyone bounced back and forth in their seats. "I would think there are some sort of precautions for these types of emergencies, Su."

"Maybe in a perfect world, but you can see it's extremely cold out there. My guess is the heating elements aren't working and its affecting the magnets. Who knows how long it's been since they've been worked on?"

"I would hope you do!" Oxford said, blasting out his words. "You must have a warranty and maintenance program for this beast—surely you wouldn't put lives at risk!"

Su shrugged. "Times are tough."

Thinking the discussion between Su and Oxford might not end well, Rachele tried to shift the attention onto something less heated. "It looks like we're inside a huge ice sculpture," she said, clutching the edge of her seat.

"She be right, mon," Jamal said, gazing out the window, "a killer one!"

"HOLD ON!" Su howled.

A deafening screech wailed through the cabin as the CyberCoaster reeled out of control. Up and down and back and forth it slid, pounding up against the tunnel walls like a sledgehammer. Shattered sheets of ice flew in all directions creating an opening for a giant tsunami of rushing water to come crashing in. Once again the Kids' Worldwide Peace Club found themselves submerged deep below the icy surface of the North Pacific Ocean. Speechless, they sat staring blankly at one another.

"Holy crap!" Ojitos slapped the seat in front of him. "We better get prepared because I'm bettin' the water temperature down here is a whole lot colder than in Jamaica!"

"Dat be a fact, mon." Jamal said, pressing his face up against the window. Da Boyz agreed with a quick nod.

It became sullen inside the coaster while the kids waited for instructions from Su. No one really knew what to say. It was a grim situation at best. Jazzi, on the other hand, was determined she was not going to let another snag in the itinerary cause her any more grief. Of course, the thought of having to fight with frizzy wet hair never made her happy.

"Over there!" Kristina yelled, breaking the silence.

The kids scrambled to the window to see what she was staring at. They became captivated by an entertaining group of sea lion pups performing acrobatics around the coaster. Watching them spin in circles and chase each other was a nice distraction from an otherwise bleak situation.

"That is just too cute." Jazzi giggled and twisted her hair.

"Too cute?" Oxford thundered. "You really think anything about our situation is *cute*, Jazzi?"

"Oh, don't overreact, Oxy." Jazzi clasped his hand. "We've been in worse situations."

"Overreacting? Now I'm overreacting? We could all die down here! Don't you get it?" Oxford squeezed his eyes so tight they became mere slits.

Jazzi shook her head, frustrated. "Just go with it."

"Fine!" Oxford huffed. "Do you realize that if something bad happened to us down here no one would ever find us? So—NO—I'm not overreacting! Not even a tiny bit! We could all die of hypothermia, and it would take a whole lot more than global warming to expose our frozen bodies." He threw his arms up in the air, irritated. "Why—WHY do I even try?" He grabbed his heart and thrust his head back.

"Who's being the drama queen now?" Jazzi fluttered her eyes, mocking him.

Oxford was worn out trying to convince Jazzi how serious their situation was, and knowing he wasn't going to change her mind, decided to press his nose up against the window and watch the pups. As much as he hated to admit it, they were kind of cute, and it was probably healthier to focus on something other than death.

The baby sea lions bobbed up and down and swam around in circles, amusing everyone as if they were performing in the circus. It was a nice contrast.

"We have some serious decisions to make," Su announced grimly.

Hayley stepped forward. "Everyone sit back in your seats and buckle up—now!"

The kids moved away from the windows and did exactly as they were instructed. They had seen firsthand that it was best to listen to Hayley.

It wasn't long before Oxford decided to throw his comments out to the group. He sat tall in his seat. "It appears to me that we are at the edge of an iceberg, which makes perfect sense, because in the northern hemisphere the ocean's surface is covered by large floating masses of ice that have detached from glaciers and then float to sea."

Finn looked up through the window to try to gauge just how deep they were. He could see the ocean floor, which didn't look promising.

"Hey!" Ojitos pointed up. "We're covered in ice, but the good news is, I don't see any more treacherous icicles!"

"It appears we've floated to the surface and are now stuck under a layer of ice," Su said despondently. He slumped back in his seat and stared at the control panel. "I'm going to try to figure a way to get back to the tunnels, but it may take me awhile."

Alarmed, Jazzi snapped, "Well, what's your interpretation of *awhile*, Su? We only have so much time you know!"

"Your guess is as good as mine," he muttered.

Oxford turned on his iNo, but just as he was about to log on, he heard a loud moan coming from outside the coaster. "Anyone hear that?"

"Ya, mon." Jamal and Da Boyz replied, nodding in unison.

"I did—unfortunately." Finn looked out the window troubled.

"What is it?" Rachele chimed in concerned.

For no apparent reason the coaster started shaking again. Su checked but couldn't figure out why. Jazzi was still peering out the window when she saw a huge shadowy figure with enormous teeth latch on to one of the sea pups and drag it down into the murky depths below.

"Oh NO!" she screamed. "What was that?"

"Looked like an orca," Su called out. "Hang on in case it tries to ram us!"

"What's an orc..."

"An orca is more commonly known as a killer whale, Jazzi," Oxford said, jumping in with his iNo, "and it's actually the largest species of the dolphin family, although people frequently mistake them for whales. They can weigh up to six tons, grow to thirty-two feet and live from fifty to one hundred years."

Oxford had barely finished speaking when he was thrown back in his seat. A devastating blow to the side of the coaster, tossed bodies about the cabin like ragdolls, causing the entire electrical system to shut down.

It was pitch black inside the coaster, but everyone remained calm. Hayley hurried about the cabin handing out flashlights and helping kids back to their seats.

"Brace yourself!" Su yelled. "We're in for another attack!" He could see the orca circling around to the nose of the coaster and then—BAM! It felt like they had been hit by a train. Su flew off his seat and was knocked to the floor unconscious. Hayley rushed to put cold compresses on his head, but he didn't respond. Nelson and Cat-Man-Doo slid sideways through the cabin and ended up under the front row of seats next to Su.

"SU'S BLACKED OUT!" Jazzi screeched, squeezing her head in despair. "Now what?"

"Someone's got to try to maneuver this thing," Ojitos cried out.

"Yes," Jazzi agreed, "but *who*?"

CHAPTER 20
A PUDDLE OF FEAR

Jazzi turned to Oxford. "You're the computer whiz here. Do something!"

"M-m-m-me?" Oxford stuttered. "I don't know anything above CyberCoasters."

"Well now's a good time to learn!" The kids joined in agreeing with Jazzi.

"C'mon, Oxy—*pleeezzz?*" She fell to her knees begging. "You're the smartest kid I know!" She looked up at him, fluttering her long eyelashes. "Out of everyone on this coaster you're probably the *only* one who can make it work!"

Oxford was taken aback by Jazzi's words.

"Tryyyyyy?" She pursed her pouty lips. "For meeeeee?"

"Oh, alright."

Realizing he was putty in Jazzi's hand and there wasn't much choice, Oxford sat down in Su's seat and stared at the panel. With quivering hands, he started pushing buttons and flipping switches.

Okay, I can do this, he thought to himself.

"I know, Oxy." Jazzi continued to schmooze him. "Pretend it's an underwater video game. Your mission is to navigate the CyberCoaster through a deadly layer of ice in order to escape the dark underwater kingdom of killer whales and conquer the new world above. You will become a superhero and win the hearts of the people." She patted him on the back.

Oxford shuddered realizing that what Jazzi had just dreamed up wasn't that far from the truth—if he was going to pull this off, he needed to focus. He sat stymied, rubbing his temples trying to figure out which button to push next.

Jazzi stood peering over his shoulder, when suddenly Ojitos rushed up behind her and whispered something in her ear. He had been observing the sights outside the window and noticed the orca was circling beneath them. It was urgent that Oxford know the killer was resuming charging position.

Fear swept across Jazzi's face—she tapped briskly on Oxford's shoulder. "Uhhh, Oxy, you might want to speed things up—NOW!"

One look at her and the pressure was on. He immediately searched around the panel and, discovering a button that read, *In Case of Water Emergency Only,* he boldly pushed it. The propellers immediately kicked in, stirring up water and emotions alike, but as the excitement mounted— Ojitos' heart sank.

"*Ay Caramba*—LOOK UP! That layer of ice is so thick! It's going to take a miracle to get through."

Oxford couldn't take his eyes off the treacherous sheet of ice daring to be cracked. *Okay, I can do this…I can do this*! He mumbled to himself, trying to drum up courage.

The kids grabbed hands, closed their eyes and braced themselves for a harsh impact. They agreed it was going to take a miracle and their only hope was to pray—each in their own personal way. Oxford took a deep breath, locked everything into place, then sat back and waited. The propellers kicked into motion—the nose of the CyberCoaster slowly lifted up. Gripping the lever with his sweaty fist, he steadily pulled back. A powerful surge of water shot out from under the coaster and launched them straight up through the ice, exposing a beautiful array of colorful crystal prisms—it was so surrealistic. The passengers gave Oxford a round of applause as the coaster skidded effortlessly across the icy surface, then slowly came to a stop. Minutes later, the monster-sized orca burst through the same hole and flew across the glacier, spraying a fountain of water as it coasted by. The kids peered out the windows in awe as it glided along the ice and landed a short distance from the coaster.

"Gud timin', mon," Jamal called out to Oxford, "dat orca cudda crushed us."

No one was sure if the killer whale was dead or alive, and there were no volunteers brave enough to venture over and check. Inside the coaster it was cold, dark, and deadly silent. Hayley removed the compress from Su's forehead—he was beginning to show signs of life. He slowly sat up and looked around, rubbing his head.

"Are we there yet?" he asked, confused.

"Yeah, well, who knows, Su? We're definitely somewhere, and we have Oxy to thank for that." Jazzi smiled fondly at Oxford and rubbed her cold hands together. "We're so happy you're back with us now but, can somebody please turn up the heat?"

Hayley hunted around for extra blankets, while Su managed to get to his feet and assess the damage. The crash had knocked out the central power again, but at least they were on solid ground.

"It be freezin', mon!" Jamal shivered. He and Da Boyz tried to bury themselves under their instruments to keep warm. This was definitely not the climate for shorts.

Nobody was prepared for the chilling weather, and with no snow gear, no heat, and no lights, it was just a matter of time before they would freeze to death.

"I know it's extremely cold," Oxford admitted, "but I think we need to go outside and try to figure out how to get off this iceberg—don't you agree Su?"

SEARCH FOR THE MISSING PEACE | 125

Su nodded. "Let's see what we're dealing with."

"Coming with us, Hayley?" asked Ojitos.

"No, I'll stay behind in my cabin like I'm assigned to do. My bodysuit is insulated and protects me from all elements."

"Humph, we should all be so lucky," Jazzi whined. She leaned over and stroked Nelson's back. "Lucky dog, you and Cat-Man-Doo have fur coats to keep you warm."

Nelson panted in agreement while Cat-Man-Doo rubbed up against Jazzi's leg.

Hayley smiled. "You'll know to plan ahead next trip." Before retreating back to the cabin, Hayley cleaned up the mess and put everything back in the first-aid kit. Then the robot marched back to the compartment with flashlight in hand. Nelson and Cat-Man-Doo trotted behind until they each found a seat to curl up on. It was safer for them to stay inside.

The kids were very nervous and unsure of what they might find on their new adventure, but willingly followed Oxford and Su outside into the grueling weather. They carefully maneuvered their way onto the iceberg, tiptoeing past the sleeping orca. The wind whipped against their faces, causing them to turn a bright stinging red. They stayed close together, cautiously taking one step at a time, hoping to remain upright as they searched the area. After walking a short way, they stopped at the base of a mountain.

"Check it out!" Ojitos said, pointing up.

"Wow! That's one big mountain!" Finn replied. "Should we climb it?"

But before anyone could answer, a gigantic ball of snow came barreling down the slope towards them. No one moved—they stood frozen, like pins at a bowling alley waiting to be struck. As the ball zoomed closer, it bounced off a ridge, flew up into the air and burst into a million sparkling snowflakes. Out sailed a kid on a snowboard, waving his arms eagerly, as he fishtailed up alongside the peace team, completely knocking them off their feet—a spray of snow slapped their faces, turning their cheeks a bright cherry red.

"STEEE-RIKE!" yelped the energetic boy. One by one, the kids jumped up and quickly brushed away the freezing snow.

"Hope no one's hurt!" he asked concerned. "But that was gnarly, dude—I slammed you!" The boy gave a friendly smile, grinning from ear to ear.

"We noticed," Jazzi sputtered, spitting out a mouthful of snow. She glared at the boy.

He had a royal blue beanie pulled down over his ears, and wore silver goggles to protect his eyes. Only his rosy cheeks and frozen nose were exposed. He held tightly onto his notepad, which he had wrapped in sealskin to keep the battery warm.

"You know you've got about sixty seconds before frostbite kicks in and you become solid citizens!"

"Huh?" Jazzi stared.

"A play on words, man. Solid means frozen, citizens are people, so solid citizens are frozen people—get it?"

"Clever," Jazzi said, perturbed.

Oxford nodded. "I like it."

"You would." Jazzi gave Oxford one of her looks.

"Okay, so let's get moving." The boy put his notepad down and pulled an emergency snow kit from his backpack. "I suggest you dudes cozy up real tight while I get this set up. This really isn't shorts weather." He rolled his eyes at Jamal and Da Boyz.

No one asked questions—they did as they were told and huddled together. Very quickly the boy had his survival kit opened and retrieved two flares and an expandable blanket. He threw a bag in the air which instantly opened up into a full-blown weatherproof tent that would protect them from the harsh elements.

"You SCORRRED!" He lifted up the flap of the tent and ushered the kids inside. "Welcome to your new abode!"

"Impressive!" Oxford said, shivering.

"We be scorin', mon!" Jamal beamed. The hairs on his legs had turned white from frostbite.

A host of grateful grins circled the tent as color began returning to chilled cheeks and slowly thawing bodies. Everyone agreed that being warm was the only thing they cared about at that particular moment.

"So how did you do that?" asked Oxford.

"Do what?" the boy replied.

"Fly down the mountain on your snowboard without losing your notepad?"

"Practice," said the boy. "Ya gotta be fast around these parts in case the village rumors are true."

"What village rumors?" Su asked.

"Ever heard of the Abominable Snowman?"

Oxford shook his head nervously and searched his iNo. "Yeah, but that's just a myth."

"Think what you want, dude—I don't plan to be hangin' in case he should just happen by. There have been sightings of an oversized creature roaming about the canyon."

"You talk like a skater not an Eskimo," said Jazzi.

"That's because I'm not an Eskimo."

"What are you then?"

"I'm a skater, brah. My name is Skawt, and I'm packed and ready to take the journey with ya to the UN."

"You mean you're the representative from Alaska?" Jazzi asked, surprised.

"That's a fact." He nodded.

"So do you need to tell your family you're leaving?"

Skawt pulled off his stocking cap. He had a cowlick that stood straight up on the crown of his head and waved back and forth in the wind. He shook his head.

"Nah, my parents are divorced. I sorta have two families: one with my dad and one with my mom. I already gave them the 'what's up' on my whereabouts. It's all good."

"Right. My parents are divorced too," Jazzi said bitterly.

Skawt grinned and gave her a high five. "Looks like we're connected."

"Yeah, we're connected alright." Her spirit dampened. "We both get to move back and forth from house to house, share two closets, two beds, and hang out with two sets of half-time friends—it SUCKS!"

"Whoaaa—relax!" Skawt backed off. "Just making friendly conversation, didn't mean to upset ya."

Suddenly an eerie shriek echoed down through the canyon walls.

"What was that?" Oxford trembled.

"Was it the whale?" Kristina asked frightened.

"Uh-oh—might be him!" Shivers ran up Skawt's spine. "Haven't heard that sound in a long time. Was hoping he was a slushy by now."

"You hoped who was a slushy?" Oxford asked.

Skawt peeked outside the tent. "The Abominable Snowman, dude—who else?"

"Right," Oxford laughed. "How gullible do you think we are?"

"Don't know." Skawt pulled his beanie over his ears as he hurried out of the tent. "I'm outta here!"

The kids stuck their heads outside to confirm Skawt's words and were shocked by what they saw. A horrific-looking creature was charging down the mountain right for them. As he came into view they could see his eyes glowing with an angry shade of red—an unbearable stench radiated from his body. The monster looked to be about ten feet tall; a massive body of blubber and dirty white fur.

"AHHHHH!" they shrieked. "The Abominable Snowman—it's REAL!" Instinctively, they grabbed their oversized blanket and bolted out of the tent.

"We believe you, Skawt!" Jazzi shouted. "WAIT UP!"

"YEAH!" Oxford panted, "Riiight…behiiind…youuu!"

Skawt was already half-way down the mountain. He tried to warn them but they wouldn't listen.

"Pick up the pace!" screeched Su, glancing behind them. "It's gaining on us!"

The CyberCoaster was in plain view now, but so was the vegged out orca. And even though the coaster was out of commission, their only hope was to climb inside and shut out their uninvited guest. It would be risky running past the whale—the last thing they needed was two behemoth beast after them. The terrain was very slippery which was making it very difficult to run.

"Help!" Kristina cried out, reaching for Rachele's hand as she plunged to the ground. Rachele hurried to grab onto Jazzi, who was holding onto Oxford and Ojitos, causing the entire group to plummet right along with her.

Finn was quick to hop to his feet, followed by Ojitos. Together they managed to pull the others up, and off they went, running as fast as they could toward the coaster. Fear brought on a sudden rush of adrenaline as the snowman roared closer and closer.

The beast was only a few feet away, charging at full speed. Skawt was already inside the coaster waiting with outstretched arms to help everyone board. Ojitos chose to straggle behind, making sure everyone was safe inside before he entered. Just as he was about to jump in, an icy white arm reached up and grabbed his leg. Fortunately, he was fast to react, and wiggled through the creature's clammy, cold fingers—escaping what could have been his final destination.

"Shut the door—HURRY!" Jazzi screamed.

"I tried to tell you," Skawt scolded them. He stood straddling the backs of two seats, one on each side of the aisle.

Ojitos laid on the floor trying to catch his breath. "Are you okay?" Jazzi asked, trying to comfort him. It took all of his strength to give her a limp thumbs-up. "That was so brave," she cooed.

"Yeah and thank goodness the orca didn't move." Finn said, feeling relieved.

But the ghastly ordeal was not over. Since the power was out, Su was having trouble closing the door. That gave the snow monster enough time to wiggle his arm inside, which instantly lead to mass hysteria. The kids went ballistic—climbing over seats and stepping on top of each other, trying to escape the huge hairy hand. Hearts were pounding so loud you could practically hear them and then—the door slammed shut.

The group sat speechless. With backs pressed to the wall and their minds racing, they gazed down horrified as the severed arm flopped about the cabin floor—still pulsating. Outside, they heard a fierce whine and then the sound of footsteps galloping off into the snowy wilderness.

"I can't look." Rachel buried her face in her arm and held onto Kristina. "The arm—is it still alive?"

"Dis kan't be 'appening, mon!" Jamal stared wide-eyed, his dreads were stiff from the freezing snow. "It still be movin'!"

'Enery stepped forward. "Shud I hit it wif my crutch?"

Cat-Man-Doo was curled up tight into an inconspicuous fur-ball next to Hayley.

"Nah, let Nelson have it," Jazzi responded. She knew he was ready to take on his new role as Warrior Dog.

"GO FOR IT, BOY!" she commanded.

Nelson leaped forward, ferociously barking. Again and again, he licked and snarled and tugged at the arm as it wriggled about the floor. One last forceful bite and it was over. The corners of Nelson's mouth dripped with melting snow. The heat of his breath had reduced the limb to nothing more than a puddle.

"D-d-did you see dat?" Kristina asked, traumatized by what she had just witnessed.

"I don't know why you didn't believe me." Skawt shrugged his shoulders and jumped down off the seats. "I can't make these things up!"

"When it got close, Skawt…," Jazzi paused.

"Go on…" Skawt motioned for her to continue.

"Did you notice the red flames in his eyes?" She shuddered.

"Yup, he's one mean dude, and for the record—missing an arm won't slow him down one bit."

"Maybe he's bipolar." Oxford rubbed his chin, pondering the possibility.

"Seriously, dude?" Skawt looked at him strangely.

"Oh please, why would you say such a ridiculous thing?" Jazzi crossed her arms. "Must you have an answer for everything?"

Oxford stood his ground. "Alright, crazy notion, perhaps. On the other hand, what if he's just lonely?"

"Lonely? Are you out of your mind?" Jazzi ranted.

"No, everyone knows that loneliness is the root of bitterness."

"Everyone, Oxy?" Jazzi clapped her hand over her forehead.

"It makes perfect sense, Jazzi. Bitterness and anger run hand in hand. I bet the creature has stored up issues that cause him to lash out and…" Oxford rambled on, barely stopping for a breath.

"STOP!" Jazzi cupped her ears. "Since when did you become a clinical researcher for disturbed snowmen?"

Oxford chose not to comment. He stood hovering over the puddle, sadly shaking his head.

Jazzi looked at Su. "Now what?"

SAVE DA WHALE, MON

Frightening details about a chase down the mountain, and Nelson's brutal attack on a gargantuan icy arm, led Hayley to grab a bucket and mop. Once the melted mess was thoroughly wiped up and the cabin restored to order, the loyal cyberite resumed the task of making everyone comfortable.

"Welcome back. I see we have a new passenger." Cyber-snacks were promptly distributed. "I will go over the rules once we're up and running, but until then, eat up. It will calm your nerves and restore your energy."

Oxford held up his cyber-snack and read the ingredients. "It's going to take more than a cookie to calm these nerves."

"Just take a bite, Oxford!" Hayley scolded him. "It worked before." The cyberite gave him a stern look and shuffled confidently down the aisle.

Oxford thought it wise to refrain from further comments until Hayley was out of range. Then he turned to Jazzi and continued to rant.

"Energy to continue on?" Oxford frowned. "Continue on to what? Another unknown mystery adventure? Please, God, no more!"

Jazzi unwrapped her snack and plopped back in her seat, exhausted. She reminded Oxford that once they were on board, they were stuck.

"You didn't forget, did you?" She pinched his elbow.

"Hrumph." Oxford shook his head. "Minutia." He slumped down in his seat and closed his eyes.

Most of the kids had already finished eating and were cozied up under blankets, enjoying their R&R. They needed time out to regroup and hash out their escape plans. Jazzi was having a hard time relaxing. Time was quickly rushing by in her mind, and she needed to complete her assignment—or else. She wasn't especially thrilled about the *or else* part.

"I hate to disturb anyone," Skawt said, gnawing on his cyber-snack, "but the e-mail I got said you would be coming to Girdwood to meet me. I wasn't expecting a wild ride on a glacier. What's up with that?"

"It wasn't exactly what we had planned," Su replied.

"No? Okay, gotcha bro—go with the flow." Skawt scarfed down the last bite of his snack.

As the kids gained their strength back, they started tossing ideas around on how they were going to get out of their current situation. But just as Ojitos was about to throw in his two cents, a loud deep moan coming from outside the coaster brought all conversation to an immediate halt.

"Is that another monster?" Kristina asked, huddling up next to her sister.

Rachele gasped. "Maybe it's the one-armed snowman back for revenge!"

"No, over there." 'Enery pointed out the window. "Did you forget about the orca? It appears to be alive."

The moans grew louder. "Oh no, it sounds like it's suffering," Kristina replied. "We should help it."

The kids wrapped up in their oversized blanket and climbed back out of the CyberCoaster. As they cautiously approached the ailing creature, they noticed there were two smaller whales that had surfaced near-by and were crying out to their companion. The *so-called* killer didn't seem quite as threatening now that she was helplessly sprawled out on the ice.

"What should we do?" Kristina asked.

"I have no idea, replied Jazzi." But don't think you can rescue it and bring it home like you did with Pookie. It makes Pookie look like a house pet." Jazzi turned to Oxford. "I bet that's the mother of those two babies."

Oxford opened his iNo. "Excuse me, Jazzi, but baby orcas are called calves."

"Well I don't care what they're called, they're babies to me," Jazzi snapped back.

"We have to do something!" Finn joined in.

"Poor thing," Rachele replied. "She looks sad."

"Poor thing?" Su scratched his head. "Sad? Are you joking? I'm pretty sure that's the same beast that attacked the coaster earlier and almost sent us to an early grave. I don't want any part of helping her. She deserves to suffer!"

"Dude, she was probably trying to protect her young," Skawt said. "We've gotta help her, man. She can only survive so long out of water, she'll become dehydrated and die.

Su threw off the blanket and stood back with his arms crossed, appalled at the thought of helping a creature that had tried to attack them earlier that day.

"C'mon, Su," 'Enery urged. "We should 'elp it. 'Tis a livin' creatur."

Ojitos nodded. "I'm in."

Jamal smiled. "You can count on me and Da Boyz."

"Oxy, you and Finn good with helping?" Skawt asked.

They both nodded eagerly.

All eyes were on Su and he was definitely feeling it. "Alright, alright, I'm outnumbered, but my hearts not in it," he confessed. "This isn't going to be an easy task, you know. Look at the size of that blubbery blob!"

"*Blob*?" Rachele replied with disgust. "That *blob* happens to be a mother with two babies."

"How insensitive of me." Su rolled his eyes. "I think there's some rope back at the coaster. Maybe we could tie it around her and drag her out to sea." He paused. "On second thought, I don't know—she's huge! I wasn't really planning on rescuing a monster." Su looked away knowing full well he wasn't scoring any points.

"C'mon, Su," Ojitos jumped in. "Let's go get the rope."

Hayley joined the boys as they searched the cabin for anything they could find that was strong enough to transport their orca friend. Su discovered two extra doors in one of the storage rooms and Ojitos suggested they connect them together to make an oversized sled. It would not only be sturdy, it would also be wide enough. The challenge, of course, would be sliding it underneath her. Su threw the rope on top of the doors and lifted one end, while Ojitos grabbed the other and off they went.

After Ojitos shared his ingenious idea, the group joined in to make it happen. In no time at all, they had created a rather impressive-looking sled capable of transporting a very large passenger—at least that's what they hoped.

Skawt stood back admiring their work. He had been put in charge of overseeing the rescue effort and was determined to make it happen. There was no backing down.

"Okay, dudes," he shouted, "let's slide 'er on up!"

The kids stared at Skawt with jaws dropped open. They had no idea how to begin this unthinkable task. Shoving a gigantic orca onto an improvised snow sled was not something they had been taught in school.

"Okay, I get it, this is new for ya." Skawt grinned. "Just listen and try to do what I say. Jamal, you and Da Boyz put your hands under her and lift her belly as high as you can. 'Enery, Finn, Su, you guys crank up the ol' rear. Ox-man, once she's off the ground a little, you, Ojitos, and the chicks hurry and start sliding the sled underneath her as far as you can go. Once the sled is under her, everyone put your muscles in gear and shove 'er into place." He stepped back and brushed his hands together. "Yup, we can do this."

Kristina slowly raised her hand to get Skawt's attention. "What if she doesn't like being pushed? What if she gets mad and rolls over on us?"

Rachele nodded. "Ya, I never thought of that. We didn't have to worry about that with Pookie."

"Yeah," Jazzi replied, "you only had to worry about being *squeezed* to death!"

"C'mon girls, no time for bantering. We're going to have to take our chances if we want to help her," Skawt said. "Okay—everyone ready?" All heads nodded yes. "Then let's do it! One, two—PUSH! Three, four—PUSH!"

"AHHHHH, keep going guys!" Jazzi belted out, straining with all her might. "We've almost got the sled in place."

"It's no use." Su stopped out of breath. "This whale ain't goin' anywhere even if we do get her on the sled. She's mammoth!"

"C'mon, Su, don't stop lifting. She's just about there," Ojitos said. "We can figure out how to move her once she's on."

The kids were determined they were going to make it work, but because the orca was semiconscious, it was like moving dead weight. Due to strong convictions and a little bit of luck, one final shove managed to maneuver the extremely large mother onto the sled.

"See, Su? We did it!" Rachele and Kristina applauded.

"Now that she's on, I've got an idea," said Oxford. "Why don't we use the CyberCoaster to push the sled?"

"Great idea, Oxy!" Ojitos gave a thumbs-up.

"Hmmm, it's possible." Su rubbed his chin. "I suppose if I put it into manual override and enter a direction, it can still work with or without the magnets."

"Go for it, Su!" the girls cheered him on.

"Ya—save da whale, mon!" Jamal and Da Boyz joined in.

Su and Oxford ran back to the coaster and climbed inside. Su positioned himself in his seat and stared at the mainframe. He scratched his head, confused.

"Hayley," he called, "can you help me out here?"

Hayley emerged from the back quarters and, after hearing Su's request, guided him step by step through the emergency startup procedure. A cyberite was well trained on what to do in emergency situations; it was clearly a critical part of the program.

"Flip that switch and punch in that coordinate," Hayley commanded. "Then push that little red button right above your head and you should be good to go." Nelson and Cat-Man-Doo stood by Hayley wagging their tails and then followed willingly as they were led back to their seats.

Su did as he was instructed and immediately the engines fired up. Su and Oxford made eye contact, but words weren't necessary.

"Whadaya say we just keep this little secret between you and me, Oxy?" Su smiled sheepishly. He was embarrassed that Oxford had witnessed how easy it was for Hayley to start the coaster when he couldn't.

"Deal, as long as you're not too proud to ask Hayley for help—that's *if* we should run into another problem." Oxford challenged him.

After the boys shook on it, Oxford ran back to help tie the ropes from the sled onto the back of the CyberCoaster. Once it was secured, the kids made their way back to their seats and prepared for the task. Since Skawt was dressed in his snowboard attire, he volunteered to stay outside and shout directions.

Su pushed the forward lever and the CyberCoaster slowly slid along the ice, heading for the hole where the calves were patiently awaiting their mother's arrival.

As the coaster drew closer to the opening, Su made an abrupt turn, causing the sled to swing out sideways in the direction where Skawt was standing. Skawt shoved the sled as hard as he could with his boot. The rope snapped in two and sent the sled sailing straight into the freezing cold water. Cheers rang out as the kids watched the mother orca bounce back to life after reuniting with her babies. As the family swam away, the kids felt good knowing they had helped. Without them, the orca never would have made it.

"That was a huge ordeal," Jazzi called out to her teammates. "But at least the whale has found some peace. What do you say we concentrate on finding our own?" Jazzi turned to Su. "By the way, I hope you know how to get us back to the tunnels via land instead of water."

Su sat frozen in his seat. Jazzi did have a point. The CyberCoaster may be up and running, but he had no clue where they were, or how to get back to the tunnels.

Skawt got up out of his seat and made his way up to Su. "So brah, thought you might need my help to get us outta here"

"What makes you think that?" Su said, insulted.

"Whoa, dude, no need to get uptight! Just know these parts like the back of my hand, and you did sort of stray off course."

"Oh, well—sure," Su admitted reluctantly. "I'm completely lost."

Overhearing the conversation, Hayley pranced forward and handed Su a map pinpointing specific locations to the emergency tunnels that led back underground.

"This will help," said the cyberite. "You just need to locate the closest module landing pad in order to enter."

"A map? Dude, those are ancient. Doesn't this thing have a navigation system?" Skawt asked.

"Of course it does," replied Su, still agitated. "But for security reasons it can't pull up emergency tunnels."

"Umm, got it." Skawt looked over Su's shoulder and began surveying the map. "Okay, you were originally planning to enter into Girdwood so…umm….there should be an entrance near there."

"That was the plan," Su nodded.

Skawt continued searching the map. "There it is!" He put his finger on the spot.

"Great, now how do we get to Girdwood from here?" Su was not being very cooperative.

"Not a prob." Skawt beamed. "You steer—I'll navigate."

After many miles of turning and sliding on the ice like a supersized Jet Ski, the CyberCoaster slid around a curve and stopped a few feet in front of a wall of snow.

Skawt pointed. "Over there—see? The good ole' town of Girdwood."

"Then according to this map," Su said, frowning, "the entrance should be…" He looked up at the massive mountain of snow looming in front of them and pointed. "There?" He gulped. "You sure that's the right spot?"

"Right on," Skawt said. "It makes perfect sense, dude, because no one ever comes here. It's too steep to get any board action. Let's go check it out."

Su shrugged. "Is there an option? Not sure I can maneuver the CyberCoaster through such a dense wall of snow."

"No worries." Skawt smiled confidently. "We'll figure it out."

Su wasn't so sure. "Attention," he announced to the passengers. "We may have found our emergency entrance back to the tunnels. Chill a few minutes while Skawt and I go survey the area. We don't need any more surprises."

"Chill? I'm done chilling," Jazzi sniveled. "Get us out of here!"

The other kids sat back in their seats contented to munch on their cyber-snacks. After all they had been through, what was a few more minutes?

It didn't take long before the two boys returned, grinning from ear to ear. Su was confident he had come up with a plan to get them back.

"I hope those grins mean we're on our way out." Jazzi said, settling back in her seat.

"Buckle up and prepare for takeoff," said Hayley, after getting the go-ahead nod from Su.

Su's mind was racing. He sat down, fastened his belt, and slowly pulled back a lever. He knew the magnets on the CyberCoaster were frozen and once the lever was in position, a spark would ignite. That would create a shaking sensation so powerful it could trigger an earthquake—at least that's what he hoped. Su locked eyes with Skawt—it was time. An uneasy rumbling, followed by a series of mild tremors, caught the kid's attention.

"What's going on, Su?" Jazzi asked nervously, feeling the ground beneath her begin to shift.

Jamal tried to stand up, but all the bouncing knocked him back in his seat. "Hey, Su, mon—sumptin' not right."

Su knew the kids were getting scared but he wasn't going to let them in on his secret plan. What if it didn't work? They might think he was crazy—he liked to think of himself as a genius.

"Stay calm," he said. "I've got it under control."

Oxford turned to Jazzi with clenched fists. "Why do those words make the hair on the back of my neck stand up?"

Unlike the passengers, Su was dizzy with excitement. The jolting motion had released waves of stored up energy that erupted violently beneath the surface. The base of the massive white wall rocked with such intensity, it literally spilt in half. Large chunks of snow cascaded down from the top like a waterfall, forming tall columns of ice along each side of the tunnel. The once intimidating barrier had suddenly transformed into a glistening archway of icicles—begging to be entered.

"Did that just happen?" Jazzi shouted, amazed by what she saw.

Kids were kneeling on their seats with their faces pressed up against the windows. It wasn't every day you got to see a mountain of snow break in half!

"You did it, Su!" Skawt jumped up and gave him a high-five. "Now let's get back to the spot you were supposed to have entered." A cacophony of cheers exploded inside the cabin.

Su smiled smugly as he pushed in the coordinates, pleased his plan had actually worked. Eagerly, he guided the CyberCoaster through the opening of the archway and spiraled his way back down to the underground tunnels. A "Welcome to Girdwood, Alaska" sign was hanging in plain view as the coaster glided up alongside the platform with the old familiar names.

Jamal laughed. "Wot kinda funny tok do dey say here, mon?"

"Yeah, look at those names?" Jazzi agreed. "Even if I was hooked on phonics, I couldn't pronounce them—well, all accept for Bob," she giggled.

Ojitos joined in laughing. "Bobs' are everywhere!"

Oxford was busy searching his iNo, but before he could come up with an answer, Skawt had already responded. "Those are Eskimo names. The actual name of the people is Inuit. It means '*those who eat raw fish*'."

"Raw fish?" Su's eyes lit up. "Sushi sounds good."

"I'm thinking Eskimo Pie," Jazzi joked, "for '*those who crave chocolate*'!"

Skawt rolled his eyes. "Good one, Jazzi."

"Genius," Su laughed as he turned up the heat. "Where to now, Jazzi?"

"Hopefully somewhere warm and peaceful!" She said shivering.

CHAPTER 22

A KID'S CABOOSE

Jazzi fumbled around for the map, her fingers were so cold she could barely open it. While everyone settled back in their seats and prepared for takeoff, she decided to take the map and move over next to Skawt. "What's up?" Skawt grinned.

"Um…I was sorta wondering…" she spoke quietly, "are you mad your parents got divorced?"

"Nah…," he moved closer. "But that's not to say I didn't think it was really bogus at first."

Jazzi looked at him puzzled. "What changed?"

He looked at her beaming. "Really want to know?"

Jazzi nodded. "Guess so."

"Okay, the truth is, I woke up one day and knew I had to forgive them."

"Forgive them?" Jazzi pulled back surprised.

"Totally! Parents are just human. They make mistakes too."

"You got that right!" she huffed.

"But their mistakes don't make them bad peeps or mean they don't love you."

Jazzi folded her arms tightly across her chest and slid down into her seat. Skawt watched her, amused.

"Could have fooled me," she pouted.

"Hey—I had to lose the 'tude first." He smiled.

"Lose the 'tude?"

"You know—give up the grudge." He tightened his seatbelt. "It seemed pretty lame at first but, what else could I do? Stay mad the rest of my life? The anger thing was like some toxic green fungus consuming my space. It didn't make me feel any better, *or* stop my parents from getting divorced."

Jazzi watched Skawt's mouth as the words continued to spill out.

"And so you forgave them—just like that?" Jazzi lifted her head, a small tear welling up in her eye. "Wait—you're not one of those weirdos who believes in God—are you?"

"Yup," Skawt nodded. "It's all good—now I'm stoked!"

"Stoked?" Jazzi asked. "Why?"

"Cause peace is sweeet!"

"Yeah?" Jazzi pondered his words.

Skawt held up his hand and gave the peace sign.

"Well, I don't think I can forgive my parents," Jazzi said defiantly.

Skawt smiled sympathetically. "I hear ya—it's not easy. Might start by forgiving yourself."

"Forgive myself?" She frowned. "Why? What did I do?"

"Don't ask me, I'm not your judge." Skawt gave her a friendly pat on the knee. "Try it—it rocks!"

Just then, Su called out, "Hey, Jazzi, still waiting for some direction."

"Oh sorry, I got sidetracked." She got up and moved back across the aisle next to Oxford, but her mind was still on Skawt. *Why on earth would you forgive someone who hurt you? That's just weird.* She spread the map out across her lap. "Let's see...where to now Mr. X?"

Su waited patiently as Jazzi scrolled her finger back and forth across the map. She stopped and looked up.

"Israel?" she read aloud to Su. "Why Israel?"

"Ahhh, Ha Aretz." Oxford nodded.

"Ha Aretz?" Jazzi repeated.

"The Land—Ha Aretz means '*the Land*' in Hebrew. Israel is a holy land, Jazzi," Oxford smiled.

"If you say so." Jazzi glanced at her watch, discouraged. "As long as it's warmer than Alaska, I'm good with it. Kick it up a notch, will ya, Su?"

"Okay, you asked for it." He pushed in the keys, and the CyberCoaster began to accelerate.

"Yeah, we be slammin'!" said Jamal, waving his fists in the air.

Oxford grabbed the cyber-sick bag and looked over at Jazzi. She had a pouty frown on her face.

"What's wrong?" he asked. "Are you worried I might get sick?"

"No, no—it's not that."

"Upset about going to Israel?"

She sat up straight in her seat and looked Oxford directly in the eyes. "Do you think I have a 'tude?"

"A 'tude?"

"Yeah…you know…a bad attitude."

Oxford thought for a moment.

"I guess that depends," he answered carefully.

She cocked her head. "Depends on what?"

"Oh, I don't know." He shrugged. "Maybe you woke up on the wrong side of the bed, or maybe you had a fight with your parents, or maybe the waves were bad, or maybe it's a bad hair day, or…"

"Okay, OKAY," she cut him off. "Got it!"

"Having a 'tude isn't all bad, Jazzi. Even I get one once in a while when…"

Unexpectedly, the CyberCoaster came screeching to a stop, practically spilling the kids out onto the platform.

"That was quick!" Oxford said, grateful he had kept everything down.

Jazzi quickly rolled up the map and stuck it in her pocket. She and Oxford were the last ones out the door. A faint "*goodbye*" could be heard in the background as Hayley wished them well. Nelson and Cat-Man-Doo stood on the seat and watched them venture off.

Ojitos was first to reach the wall and point out the "Welcome to Israel" banner. His eyes dropped below the banner to the names written underneath and his mouth fell open.

"Moses was here? Are you kidding me?" He reached out and touched the wall. "The same Moses from the Bible?"

Oxford grabbed his chest and sighed. "And Albert Einstein?" he whispered reverently. "My hero!"

"Riiight on!" Skawt gleamed and pointed to more names. "Let's not forget the Marx Brothers, dudes."

Jazzi rolled her eyes. "Okay, guys, we're wasting precious moments here. Su, just how much time do we have, anyways?"

Su checked his phone. "Twelve hours until the United Nations closes for the weekend."

"Then let's go!" Jazzi insisted.

The group was excited as they gathered into the module and rose to the surface. The doors opened up onto a dry, dusty land dotted with palm trees and camels.

"I say we take this road," Jazzi said, holding her hand up to her forehead, staring off into the distance. The kids were fine with that since there was only one road to choose from. They followed Jazzi a short distance down a smooth dirt path and stopped at the entrance of a country farm. A friendly group of local kids were waiting out front to greet them. One of the boys was a short, well-fed Jewish boy, wearing a yarmulke on top of his head. He carried a notepad under his arm, which suggested he may be their representative.

"Shalom!" he said. "I'm Abraham, but my friends call me Abe. I would like to go with you to the United Nations."

"Excuse me," Rachele said. "What is that you're wearing on your head?"

"Oh," Abraham touched his head, "it's a yarmulke, pronounced ya-ma-ka." He pronounced each syllable slowly. "I'm Jewish and I wear this skullcap to show my respect for God. It is part of our faith," he stated proudly.

"Where are we, Abe?" Jazzi asked. "Is this a ranch, a dairy, or what?"

"It's all of that," said Abraham. "There's a school here too. We call it a kibbutz."

"A caboose?" Jazzi repeated.

"Not a caboose," Oxford chuckled, "a kibbutz. It's a communal farm. Everyone works together as a team."

"Is beeuuutiful, mon!" Jamal and Da Boyz chimed in together.

"What's that lake over there?" Jazzi stared.

"It's the Sea of Galilee," Abraham answered.

"Really?" Ojitos gazed at the lake in wonder. He remembered stories his grandmother had read him from the Bible about the Sea of Galilee. It awed him to think he might be walking on the same historical dust as Jesus.

"Abe, why would you ever want to leave this place?" Kristina asked. "It seems so peaceful."

Abraham's face darkened. "Here perhaps, but not so far away it's like a different world." He turned to Jazzi and gently squeezed her arm. "Do we have time for one more stop? I want to show you another side."

She hesitated, biting her lip. "Is it *really* important?"

Abraham nodded his head. "Seeing is believing."

"Well, I guess if it's not too far off course." Jazzi studied the map. "That's odd," she rubbed her eyes, "I just saw the X move." A chill ran up her spine as she glanced up at the storm clouds darkening the sky above them.

CHAPTER 23

THE WHINE OF REVENGE

A clap of thunder, followed by a light sprinkling of raindrops, spilled out of the sky and onto the kids as they raced back to the CyberCoaster. Once inside, Jazzi notified Su of the recent change in plans. He was getting used to surprises so he didn't question her. Abraham handed Su the new itinerary and off they sped, winding their way through a series of hidden side tunnels that veered off from the main track. After what seemed like a very short ride they pulled up to their new destination and prepared for departure.

Abraham quickly hastened to his feet ahead of the others. He motioned for Jazzi to join him as he scooted up beside Su.

"Excuse me," he spoke softly into Su's ear, "if I may, I'd like your permission to speak to the group before we exit the coaster. There are some things they need to know."

Su looked at Jazzi and shrugged his shoulders. "I don't have a problem with it, do you?"

"I'm good," she replied.

"Thank you both." Abraham nodded and stepped to the front of the cabin. "Please, may I have your attention?" Everyone stopped what they were doing and gave Abraham their undivided attention. He spoke solemnly as he faced his audience. "I need you to be ready for what you might see today."

The young travelers were all ears, curious to hear what he was about to say.

"I have brought you to an area that is in the heat of conflict," he began. "We must be prepared."

"Prepared?" Oxford whispered to Jazzi. "Prepared for what? More absurdities?"

"Shhh—let him speak."

Abraham's eyes circled the cabin, making eye contact with everyone present. Slowly he looked up. "I believe that what you're about to see will help you understand why our peace assignment is so critical."

"Critical? It's only a homework assignment," Su smirked.

Abraham stopped and looked over his shoulder at Su. "I know it may be hard to understand, but it's much more than a simple homework assignment. You may change your mind after you see what I'm about to show you."

Su smiled amusingly. Nothing he had seen so far had shown him peace was even a reality—why would it suddenly become so critical?

Abraham turned his head back and continued to speak. "As we move outside, I ask that you form a single line and follow my lead at all times. If at any time I sense danger, I will insist that you retreat back to the coaster immediately! For your own safety it is imperative that you heed my instruction." Abraham walked toward the exit. "Ready?"

"Who put 'im in charge?" 'Enery said, poking Finn. Finn was too busy tugging at his wedgie to reply.

"Finn?" 'Enery poked him again.

"Oh sorry, I was trying to…"

But before Finn had a chance to finish, a loud distant rumbling shook the tunnel, forcing pieces of rock and debris to spray across the roof of the CyberCoaster. 'Enery was quick to duck, thinking the glass top might shatter and come crashing down on top of them.

"Umm, rethinkin' wot I jus sed. We bet'er trus 'im!" His pale face stared up at the ceiling.

Finn nodded his head, agreeing.

The disturbing noises erupting so soon after Abraham's words had the kids very concerned. Exchanging worried glances, they stepped outside the coaster and rallied behind him as he guided them through a narrow opening inside one of the cave walls. It was quite dark, so they were forced to feel their way through the tunnel, until they reached an old wooden door.

"Ewe, creepy," Rachele squealed as she smacked a spider off her arm.

"Shhh," Abraham whispered, "we must be quiet."

Telltale signs made it obvious the primitive-looking door had been there for a really long time. It was rusty and weathered and completely infested with termites. A tangle of spider webs highlighted the white peeling paint that had turned a dingy yellow from years gone by.

Ojitos nudged Oxford. "Looks like nobody's been down here for a while."

"It's fascinating." Oxford held up his iNo and scrolled through a series of pictures. "Check this out, Ojitos—the door resembles an ancient relic."

"Is it an entrance to a tomb?" Ojitos asked.

"Tomb?" Kristina shivered. "Are there bodies down here?"

"No," Abraham assured her, "this is no tomb. It's just a very dilapidated door with lots of history."

"Phew!" Kristina uttered a sigh of relief.

"Spiders!" Rachele screamed, walking into a mesh of cobwebs.

Finn and 'Enery were quick to untangle the net and help her move on.

One by one the group stepped through the mysterious doorway and climbed up an old stone staircase. Unlike the module, it seemed like it took forever to reach the top. Once they arrived, Abraham explained that they were at a remote spot near the sacred Temple Mount, located in the Old City of Jerusalem. The group stood huddled together alongside a sharp embankment and peered through portals in the massive rocks. Their eyes scanned the landscape, carefully studying each detail, when an immense wall grabbed their attention.

"What's that?" Jazzi asked, wide-eyed.

Oxford scrambled through his iNo, but Abraham was way ahead of him.

"It's the Wall, Jazzi—the Western Wall. Some people refer to it as the Wailing Wall. It's a sacred spot where people come from all around the world to pray."

"I've heard about that," said Oxford, putting his iNo down. "People write prayers on small pieces of paper and stick them in between the cracks of the wall."

"But wait—who are those guys?" Jazzi pointed. "They're not praying, they're throwing rocks and fighting with each other. It looks more like a war zone!"

Just as Jazzi witnessed, gangs of young men were running wildly through the streets. Some of them had pieces of cloth wrapped around their faces, while others wore camouflage fatigues. They screamed and shouted at each other in a language the kids couldn't understand— but there was no mistaking the anger in their voices.

"Listen…" Su interrupted. "I hear gunfire!"

"Me too," confirmed Oxford, trembling. "It sounds like firecrackers bursting on the Fourth of July!"

Ojitos elbowed Jamal. "Look—over there," he said. "They're overturning cars and lighting tires on fire!"

Bright balls of orange flame engulfed in columns of black billowing smoke spiraled thickly toward heaven.

"I don't understand, Abe," Jazzi said, confused. "What are they doing?"

"The same thing they've been doing for three thousand years," he answered. "Children are taught to take revenge for their fathers' deaths. People have been fighting over this land for centuries. Generation after generation, the cycle of hate continues."

He shook his head sadly. "It's a never-ending war."

Suddenly there was a loud explosion and rocks and debris came raining down on top of them. Instinctively they ducked and covered their heads, pressing their bodies flat against the ground.

"Everybody stay down and don't move!" Abraham whispered fiercely.

Just as Abe had instructed, the kids lay motionless, not moving a muscle. Jazzi, unable to contain her curiosity, peeked up just in time to see a wounded boy dragging himself from the site of the explosion. Her stomach sank as she watched him struggle. She wanted so much to help, but she was scared. She looked at Oxford, then at Ojitos, but everyone was too afraid to move.

Then, from out of nowhere, a dark shadow of a man crept toward them. He had on army fatigues with a hat drawn low over one brow. Jazzi huddled near the ground—her teeth chattered with fright as she watched the black silhouette advancing toward her. She was just about to let out a bloodcurdling scream when the man lifted his head enough for her to get a glimpse of his eyes—his *familiar* blue eyes.

"Sir Sean?" Jazzi called out discreetly. "Is that you?"

He gave a slight nod.

"It can't be." She rubbed her eyes. "I must be hallucinating."

"No time for small talk," he said sternly. "Get back to safety." He turned and ran off in the direction of the wounded boy.

"Oxford," Jazzi spoke softly. She crawled on her belly, inching her way up beside him. "I just saw Sir Sean!"

"What?" Oxford whispered back, irritated. "This is no time for joking, Jazzi."

"No, I saw him. I swear!"

"But that's impossible. He disappeared in the clouds."

"I know, but trust me—he's back!"

Oxford buried his head underneath his arms. He wasn't sure if he believed Jazzi or not. It wouldn't be the first time she tried to prank him.

There was a heaviness in the air—Abraham carefully surveyed their surroundings. Once he saw an opportunity to escape back to the coaster, he ordered the kids to head back down the stairs pronto. They quickly rose to their feet and did as they were told. Sir Sean appeared a moment later behind them, cradling the hurt boy in his arms. Both Jazzi's and Oxford's eyes nearly popped out of their heads as they stood before him, marveling. It really was him, but what could they say? Who would believe them anyways?

"There's no time to waste," said Sir Sean. "This boy needs help." He stepped inside the coaster and cautiously laid the boy's frail body across a row of seats. Nobody bothered to question him or even ask his name. Whoever he was, they were grateful he was there to help. Hayley grabbed the first-aid kit and applied pressure to stop the bleeding. The kids stared at the boy in silence.

Jazzi's eyelids drooped. "This doesn't make sense," she said. "Why do I feel like I'm the one whose been wounded?"

CHAPTER 24

WAIL OF AGONY

S adly," Sir Sean explained to Jazzi, "everyone bleeds when a child gets hurt."

Abe hung his head and sighed. "Oy vey, back and forth it goes. An Israeli child is injured one day, a Palestinian the next."

Oxford couldn't hold back his questions any longer—he needed answers. He walked over and stood beside Sir Sean, hoping not to draw attention from the others.

"Sir Sean, you must tell me. Where did you come from? How did you get here? Why are you here? And why are you wearing military clothes instead of your pirate getup? I don't get it."

Sir Sean looked Oxford directly in the eyes. "Don't replace trust with logic, young man."

Oxford wasn't sure what he meant but knew this wasn't the time or place. Sir Sean was preoccupied with the hurt boy. Once Hayley had completed bandaging his wounds and Sir Sean felt assured he was in good hands, he darted for the exit.

"Wait, don't leave!" Jazzi yelled, running after him.

"Stop." Oxford tried to grab her. "You don't know where he's going. You might get hurt!"

Jazzi shoved his hand away and dashed out of the coaster.

"Sir Sean!" she called again, but he was too far away to hear. She continued chasing him up the staircase, panting out of breath. She skipped over as many steps as she could until she reached the top, but when she spotted him, she stopped dead in her tracks. Several men with machine guns were closing in on him. He was trapped in the middle with no way out. Without hesitation, Jazzi turned and raced back down the stairs to get help.

"JAMAL!" she screamed, rushing through the door. "Sir Sean's in trouble! You and Da Boyz…" she paused to catch her breath, "grab your instruments and come with me. I've got an idea—HURRY!"

Except for Oxford, no one knew who Sir Sean was—still no questions were asked. He was obviously someone important to Jazzi, and that was all that mattered. Jamal and Da Boyz quickly followed Jazzi back up the staircase, lugging their instruments behind them. Once they reached the top, they found a spot to hide and prepared for action. They could see the soldiers had Sir Sean surrounded—their guns aimed directly at him. Jazzi covered her eyes, too afraid to look, but then she remembered the pirate ship stunt.

If ever there was a time to disappear, she thought to herself, *it's now!*

"Jamal," Jazzi whispered fiercely, "play something and play it loud— *really* loud!"

Without another word, Jamal and Da Boyz started playing their instruments as loudly and obnoxiously as they could. Guitars wailed, drums pounded, horns blew. The diversion was working. The machine gunners stepped back surprised, dropped their weapons and grabbed their ears—the noise was excruciating. High and low the soldiers hunted, searching in and around every corner for the deafening sounds, but it was no use. They became so distracted by all the commotion they didn't notice Sir Sean slip away.

As soon as Jazzi realized he was gone, she helped the band pick up their instruments and hightail it back to the CyberCoaster—dodging bullets all the way. She knew that once the soldiers figured out they had been duped, they would be out for revenge.

It wasn't easy getting back down the narrow staircase without banging the instruments on the walls, but they managed to get back with only a few minor scratches. Now safe inside the coaster, Jazzi threw up her arms and shrieked, "HIT IT, SU!" The doors instantly slammed shut and swiftly they slid away. The sounds of running footsteps and exploding gunfire echoed in the background.

Jazzi sat down next to Oxford and buried her head in his chest. "He's *gone*."

"Gone? Sir Sean?" Oxford's chin dropped. "You mean gone *forever*?"

"I'm not sure." She stared up in disbelief.

"Wonder if this was just some sneaky way of spying on us?" Oxford tapped on his chin pondering the idea.

"*What*? He just risked his life to save Hakim. He's a hero, not a spy!"

"Good point." Oxford hated not knowing the facts.

The kids were stunned by what they had just encountered. A dismal silence filled the air—words were unnecessary. Up until now violence was something they had only seen in movies or on television. Peace suddenly took on a whole new meaning.

After some time had passed, Jazzi decided to get up and go see if she could help the injured boy. Several committee members had already gathered around him, trying to make him comfortable. They could sense the fear in his eyes as he lay peering up at them from his bloodstained clothes.

"Don't worry." Jazzi tried to console him by patting his shoulder. "You're safe with us now." She looked at Hayley hoping for some comforting words because, truth be known, she had no idea if they were safe or not.

Hayley gave Jazzi a reassuring smile then continued on with business. "There's a motorized wheelchair to help you get around while you're healing." Hayley pointed to a closet in the back of the cabin.

"Thank you," the boy said, forcing a smile.

"You're very brave," said Jazzi. "Do you remember what happened?"

He looked up at Jazzi, dazed, struggling to speak. "I remember telling my family I was going to see a friend. What I didn't tell them was that he's my new friend from Israel, and we were finally going to meet."

"Why didn't you tell them?" Jazzi asked.

"They wouldn't understand."

"But what if something worse had happened and you never made it home? They would be worried sick." Jazzi thought about her own parents and how she hadn't bothered to tell them where she was going.

"Let him finish his story, Jazzi," Oxford interrupted.

"I got on my bike and was headed to our meeting spot when, from out of nowhere, came an awful-sounding blast. It was like, I don't know, maybe a bomb exploding. Then I remember feeling a horrible pain shooting through my body and . . ." He stopped talking and buried his face in his shirtsleeve. It was hard to hold back the tears, despite the embarrassment.

"It's okay," Jazzi encouraged him. "What's your name?"

"Hakim," he moaned.

"Hakim?" Abraham repeated. "Did you just say Hakim?" He walked over and handed the boy a tissue to wipe his eyes. "Is it *you*, Hakim? Is it really *you*?"

Hakim looked up at Abraham, confused.

"It's me—Abe," said Abraham, extending his arms. "I'm Abraham, your friend!"

Hakim stared into Abraham's face tearfully and cried out, "My friend?"

Abraham bent down and gave Hakim a hug then turned toward the others. "Hakim and I knew this would be a dangerous meeting, but I didn't expect him to get hurt." He hung his head sadly. "We met through your website and have been e-mailing back and forth against our parents' wishes. We respect their desires, but we made a pact to help our people find peace. We thought it would be a good thing to meet and join with you in your quest. More than anything we want peace."

Abraham sat down next to Hakim and placed his hand on his shoulder. "Do you want to continue on my friend?"

Hakim nodded, groaning in pain. "We made a pact—there's no turning back."

Su sat at the control panel pondering Abe's words. He now understood why this mission was critical to him—it was about saving lives!

Jazzi looked over at Oxford, troubled. "Do you think we will ever find the secret to peace?"

CHAPTER 25
WAR ON WEDGIES

T his assignment is turning out to be much harder than I thought," Oxford admitted. His iNo could only do so much.

Jazzi felt very empty inside. She flopped back in her seat and slowly moved her finger across the map—fighting to hold back the tears. It was hard to concentrate after what she had just seen. She decided to try sending up a silent prayer for guidance. Maybe Skawt was actually on to something. He seemed pretty mellow so he must be getting inside information from a reliable source. Besides, at this stage of the journey, there was nowhere else to turn. She finished saying what she needed to say then slowly opened her eyes. To her amazement—there was her answer—glowing over New York City like a beacon in the night!

"New York." Jazzi lit up. "The X is on New York! It's time!" She stood up holding onto the back of her seat with one hand, and waving the map with her other. A noticeable boost in spirits resurfaced once the kids knew they were nearing their final destination. Oxford remained very still, struggling to overcome his queasiness.

"Aren't you excited, Oxy?" Jazzi grabbed his shoulders and shook him back and forth, but he didn't respond. "Oxy, did you hear me? We're scheduled to launch."

"Yeah, yeah—don't touch me."

"Really?" Jazzi pulled back frowning.

"Really, Jazzi. Unfortunately, my cyber-snack wants to launch ahead of schedule." His face turned a pale shade of gray as he leaned over holding his stomach.

Jazzi buried her head. "Oh no—I can't watch!"

"I feel for ya, Oxy." Finn grimaced as he tugged at his leather pants. "But at least you don't have wedgie issues." He scooted around in his seat fidgeting, trying to find a comfortable position and then finally—he had had enough. He unfastened his seat belt and jumped up on his seat, yelling at the top of his lungs, "I'm DONE with WEDGIES—DO YOU HEAR ME—DONE!"

A round of applause thundered through the CyberCoaster. Everyone agreed that Finn should lose the lederhosen in exchange for a pair of jeans. The problem was, no two kids could come to terms on which brand of jeans he should get. Each kid believed that his or her own personal favorites were the best. Jazzi couldn't believe anyone would challenge her since she was the fashion queen. And so it began…loud bickering back and forth, mixed with petty comments and unkind words. In a matter of minutes, it had erupted into an all-out war! Nelson and Cat-Man-Doo retreated to Hayley's cabin seeking shelter from the unnecessary pandemonium.

"I say get skinny jeans!" shouted Su.

"No way, brah," Skawt whooped. "I say go loose—let 'em hang dude!"

"I'm sorry," Rachele piped up. "It's Calvin or nothing."

"So what do you know," Finn argued. "You're just a girl!"

Kristina was fuming. "Girl's rule, Mister Fidgety, and for your information—I wouldn't be caught dead wearing lederhosen. I have my *own* style!"

"That's right," Rachele said in a snit. "Her style is to copy me!"

"Do NOT!" Kristina retaliated.

"Do SO!" Rachele jabbed her in the side.

"OW!" Kristina turned away and crossed her arms. "I only copy you…" she peered back over her shoulder, "…when I wanna keep da boys away!"

"HUH?" Rachele squealed. "No you do not!"

"Ya, it's true," Kristina argued. "And you have to wear da stretchy Calvin's because they're da only ones dat fit your big booty"

The sisters continued to hurl insults at each other, along with an occasional shove. Jazzi stepped in between them, grabbed each one by the arm and spun them around. "Neither one of you knows what you're talking about. Jeans aren't jeans unless they look like *mine*." She put her hand on her hip and struck a model pose, making a slight turn sideways. "Check these out—I'm the 'jean queen' and if you had an eye for fashion, you'd agree I'm right."

"'Tis bloody ridiculous." 'Enery waved his crutch. "I take wot I can dig out of the rubbish bin and like it."

Oxford, who was feeling much better now, attempted to enter into the conversation. "Well in my opinion . . ." His voice was instantly drowned out by a chorus of angry shouts.

Jazzi swung around with both fists in the air. "Nobody asked for your opinion!" Her face turned bright red with anger. "Have you forgotten that I'm *your* fashion advisor?"

"Well, no, but…" Oxford hung his head.

"Exactly!" Jazzi ranted, inches from his face.

"Jazzi be right, Ox mon." Jamal interrupted him. "Yor polyester duds ar almos' as bad as da Fidgety mon's pants—dey bof gotta go."

"So what do you know about what's cool or not?" Ojitos yelled at him. "All you ever wear is baggy ole shorts with creepy skeleton heads!"

Everyone was arguing and throwing their comments in. On and on it went, escalating into a contest to see who could outdo the other by being the meanest. No one would give in—they all thought *their* opinion was right.

Haley heard the arguing and came rushing out. "Oh my, so many angry faces. Perhaps you should rethink your mission. Peace? Tsk, tsk!" And with a disappointed face, the cyberite returned immediately to the cabin.

"Yup!" Su scoffed and rolled his eyes. "Can't fool Hayley."

"Okay, dat be enough." Jamal stood up, realizing someone had to take charge of the messy situation. "Everyone back off—NOW!"

It became extremely quiet. The kids stared down at the floor or out the window. They were too embarrassed to look at each other.

Abe took a seat next to Hakim, shaking his head in disgust. "Jeans sorta pale in contrast to what you've been through."

Hakim nodded. "The truth is, I'm thankful I still have legs. I don't care which brand I stick them in."

Jazzi overheard Hakim's comment and immediately leaned over to Oxford. "Did you hear that? We were so caught up arguing over our jeans that we forgot about Hakim!"

Oxford scratched his head, perplexed. "Yeah—what just happened?"

"Who knows?" she replied, hanging her head, discouraged. "Some peace committee we are. All this arguing and yelling reminds me of home."

Oxford turned to Jazzi with a look of concern. "Be honest—is this adventure more about you wanting to get your parents back together or acing your homework assignment?"

Jazzi pivoted her head so Oxford couldn't see her face. "Well—maybe it's both. I mean, nothings the same anymore. Mom's always stressed out and mad, yelling at me for no reason. I can't seem to do anything right and when dad comes to get me, all they do is argue and scream at each other—it makes me crazy!" Jazzi wiped her eyes and turned back to Oxford. "What if I could make them proud of me? What if I could actually find the answer to peace? Maybe then they would get back together and we could be a family again!"

"That would be nice, Jazzi." Oxford pushed back a wet curl from her cheek. "But just remember, even if we do find the answer to peace, there's no guarantee they'll listen."

Finn stood up and looked around at all the somber faces. "This is all my fault. I never meant to start a wedgie war."

"Nah." Oxford slapped him on the back. "It's everyone's fault. We let a minor little difference of opinion get out of control and turn into a major battle."

"Yeah," Ojitos agreed. "That's how real wars are created. How can we expect adults not to disagree over important matters when we argue over stupid meaningless stuff?"

"Exactly, dude," Skawt jumped in. "We sound more like a bunch of campaigning politicians than a peace club."

"Uh-huh," Kristina nodded. "Doesn't it make more sense to accept the fact we're all different?"

"Ya," Rachele agreed. "It would be boring if we were all the same."

"Dats right, mon," Jamal agreed, "an who cares abou' da jeans anywaz cuz dey all be cut from da same denim. It mak no difference, jeans ar jeans." Then he closed his mouth and said no more.

Without thinking, Jazzi sprang up from her seat and blurted, "Jamal's right! Plus, I've had my share of wedgies, so I know you can get one just as easily wearing jeans as you can wearing lederhosen!" Immediately, she sat down and covered her face with her hands. With fingers slightly parted, she peeked through and whispered to Oxford, "Did I just say that?"

CHAPTER 26

WHERE'S THE PEACE?

O xford nodded his head and reached over to pat Jazzi on the knee. "It's not the first time you've embarrassed yourself, Jazzi, and I'm sure it won't be the last."

Jazzi threw him a dirty look and pulled her knee away. "Is that supposed to make me feel better?" She slid as far down in her seat as she possibly could, leaned her head on the edge of the window and stared outside. The CyberCoaster whirled onward, racing past tunnel walls streaked with vibrant shades of fuchsia and periwinkle blue. It didn't take long for Jazzi's mood to switch from pangs of regret to feelings of joy once she realized she would soon be in New York City—their final destination.

"Hey!" She popped up in her seat. "I was just thinking . . ."

"Thinking?" Oxford whooped. "As in *thinking* before you speak?"

"I'm serious." She shook her finger at him. "I'm thinking we're not prepared to present our case to the United Nations. We don't know what we're going to say, or who's going to say it?"

"Say what?" Oxford frowned.

"Exactly," Jazzi replied. "We have no message, or anyone to deliver it."

"There's a message?" Su mumbled sarcastically.

Oxford shrugged. "Hmmm, hate to admit it, but you're right Jazzi."

Suddenly the cabin door flew open and Hayley's head poked out. "For your convenience, there's a conference area in the back of the coaster for brainstorming." The door closed as quickly as it had opened.

"Amazing how that cyberite always knows what we need before we do." Jazzi said, scrunching up her nose.

Su grinned. "That's its job."

"Okay, so let's put our heads together and come up with a game plan!" Jazzi hollered.

Jamal saluted her. "Sounds gud to me, mon."

Su put the CyberCoaster on autopilot and led the committee back to a large round table, where they sat tossing ideas back and forth. But despite their team effort, they still felt unprepared.

"This is more difficult than I thought." Oxford repositioned his glasses. "We only have one shot to get it right."

"I vote for Jazzi to deliver the message," Ojitos shouted.

"Me?" Jazzi gasped.

"Why not?" Su nodded.

"Um—well?" Oxford cringed. "I'm not sure…"

"No—it's agreed!" Ojitos shouted.

"Well, if everyone agrees," Oxford conceded, "guess I'm in."

"But, but—WAIT," Jazzi stammered.

"No buts about it," Ojitos said with a grin. "It's unanimous!"

"Well—okay, but—ME? Are you sure? How will I know what to say to a bunch of UN guys in suits?"

"Trust me, Jazzi, you'll dream up something," Oxford said, snickering. "You always do."

Jazzi crossed her arms and threw him one of her looks. He responded with a slight wave and devilish grin.

"Okay," Hayley said, popping out again. "We'll be landing shortly. Everyone back to your seats."

Jazzi felt both giddy and queasy, now that they were finally landing. All this time the only thing she had cared about was getting to New York. Now that they had arrived, she felt awkward and unsure of herself. Questions kept popping up in her head . . . *Should I really be the designated speaker? Am I qualified to make a presentation?*

According to Su's watch it was now 1:00 p.m. on Friday, and the CyberCoaster was just about to arrive.

"WOO-HOO!" hollered Jamal. "Dat waz sum ride, Su!"

"Yes!" Ojitos gave a thumb-s up. "The Big Apple."

Oxford, busy playing with his iNo, noted that the inside of the tunnel looked very similar to the inside of a New York subway.

"I wouldn't know," said Jazzi, pressing her nose up against the window, straining to see the wall, "I've never been in one, but…," she stopped and shouted, "…check out those names! Thomas Edison, Leonard Bernstein, Teddy Roosevelt, Houdini . . ." She turned toward Oxford and repeated, "Houdini? We may need a magic trick or two to complete this assignment." She let out a deep sigh.

Oxford wasn't paying much attention, he was too busy imagining that he might be actually sitting in the same seat that Thomas Edison once sat in, or any one of the other great minds that had come before him.

After the coaster was completely stopped, Hayley stood at the door wishing each young peace seeker good luck as they set off on their final journey. Jazzi appreciated the extra pat on the back. She needed all the encouragement she could get. One by one the kids stepped inside the module and braced themselves for the unknown. They soon found themselves standing in the middle of a quiet little grassy green park.

Jazzi was first to spot a sign that read "Peace Park". She smiled contentedly as the brisk spring air hit her face.

Abraham walked beside Hakim as he maneuvered his wheelchair next to the sign.

"Peace Park," he said, grinning down at Hakim. "Land of possibilities?"

"Why not?" Hakim nodded. "All things are possible."

"Sweet!" Skawt reached over and gave him a high five.

Just then the traffic light across the street turned green and a surge of noisy rush-hour traffic vibrated through the park: horns honked; whistles blew; impatient people scurried about pushing and shoving.

"Geez…" Jazzi said, holding her head. "Where's the *peace*?"

"Is tha' a trick question?" 'Enery asked.

"Hey," Finn piped up, "I'd like to see the Statue of Liberty."

"Yes," Oxford agreed. "It's close to where the Twin Towers once stood."

"Twin Towers?" Jazzi shook her head sadly. "If only we'd had the answer to peace back then."

"It's not too late. We can still do something," Ojitos reassured her.

"I hope so. Let's get to the United Nations and find out," Jazzi said anxiously.

"As long as the delegates are still in session," Su interjected, "we should be good to go."

"It's the getting in part that worries me," Jazzi responded.

"If we sneak in they'll have to listen to us," Ojitos replied devilishly.

"Jus stick ta gethah, mon, and we be fine," Jamal added.

With that, the team took off running. Jazzi led the way down First Avenue, with Nelson and Cat-Man-Doo prancing beside her. Abraham jogged alongside Hakim's wheelchair, while 'Enery stood on the back swinging his crutch. Oxford, Su, Ojitos and Skawt were next and bringing up the rear were the two sisters, Finn and, last but not least, Jamal and Da Boyz—it was quite a parade. They had heard New York was a busy place, but the Kids' Worldwide Peace Club was determined to make it to the United Nations building as scheduled. Swerving and dodging around herds of people, they continued to forge their way down the sidewalk.

"This reminds me of Alaska," Skawt observed. "People roaming about like migrating caribou."

"Caribou? That's weird, reminds me of my closet of shoes." Jazzi thought back on her encounter with the sole man.

"Shoes? What do shoes have to do with anything?" Su asked, confused.

"Really, Su? Think about it. Shoes come in all sorts of sizes, shapes, and colors, and they have souls—just like people!"

The kids stared blankly.

"Oh, c'mon people—shoes have soles? People have souls?" She shrugged her shoulders. "Aw, never mind, guess you had to be there."

Unsettled glances flew back and forth as the kids tried to decipher Jazzi's crazy logic. They became so distracted that, despite the blaring horns and squealing tires, no one realized they were crossing the street on a red light.

"STOP!" yelled a big burly policeman, frantically waving his club. "What do you kids think you're doing? You can't just step out in the middle of the street whenever you feel like it! You're going to cause an accident!" He pressed his lips down tightly on his whistle, and sprang into action.

"Uh-oh," Ojitos said, turning to the others, "he's AFTER us!"

"RUN!" Jazzi yelled. "We don't have time to explain!"

"Oh this is NOT good!" Oxford said, nervously wringing his hands.

Su watched as the policeman drew closer. "No choice—MOVE IT!"

With no time to think, the group panicked and took off running. The pavement seemed to stretch out endlessly as the policeman sprinted after them in relentless pursuit. He had almost reached them when, out of the blue, a trash truck came barreling around the corner and cut him off. The kids saw this as an opportunity to sneak down a back alley and duck out of view. An old trash bin, spilling over with garbage, became the perfect hiding place.

"Whew, that was close," Ojitos said, relieved.

"Yeah," Hakim gasped. "I thought my wheelchair was going to endo!"

"You an me bof!" 'Enery said, hopping off the back.

Jamal and Da Boyz did their best to squeeze in and make themselves less noticeable, but it was not a pleasant spot. Garbage fumes assaulted their noses, and rats let out short shrill squeaks as they scurried about, circling in and out between their legs.

"This brings back vivid memories of England." Jazzi held her nose and poked 'Enery. After several minutes had elapsed, she peeked out from behind the dumpster, but immediately pulled back when she saw the policeman blaze past.

After a few more minutes she tried again. "Okay, the coast is clear. Follow me, guys."

Cautiously they trailed Jazzi out the back of the alley and headed on their way.

Several city blocks into their walk Kristina stopped and shouted, "Look!" Her eyes lit up like lightbulbs as she pointed to a large building. "Is that it? Is that the United Nations?"

"Wow!" Jazzi cried out, stopping dead in her tracks. The entire peace committee went plowing into the back of her, knocking her to the ground.

"Ouch!" She picked herself up. "Watch where you're going."

"Well," Kristina repeated, "is it or isn't it?"

"That's it!" Jazzi replied. She stood gazing up in wonderment. "It's got to be."

There it was—the United Nations—standing before them like a sacred shrine. Jazzi was sure that the key to their entire mission was waiting to be unveiled somewhere inside those large ominous walls. A single beam of sunshine streamed down through a backdrop of billowy white clouds, focusing on the grand structure like a spotlight on a stage. In front of it were rows of multicolored flags, snapping and rippling in the wind. Each flag represented a different country from around the world—it was breathtaking.

"We'll soon have our answer," Jazzi said assuredly, "the *one* we've been searching for."

"Or *will* we?" Su countered with a raised eyebrow.

Jazzi was just about to reply when she heard a voice calling out her name. Her eyes darted to the left, and then to the right—who would be calling her? She didn't know anyone in New York. Again, she heard her name, only louder this time. As she scanned the area, her eyes spotted a pair of piercing blue eyes peering at her through a flurry of flapping wings.

"No way!" She squinted and took a second look. "Sir Sean?" She rubbed her eyes. "Are you kidding me?"

Although he was now clean-shaven and dressed in a dark navy blue suit with a contrasting paisley green tie, his kind blue eyes were undeniable. The fact that he was surrounded by an assortment of birds was also a good indication.

Jazzi walked closer. "It is you! What are you doing here? You show up at the strangest times!"

Sir Sean grinned and lifted his arm to motion Jazzi closer. Instinctively, the birds burst into a kaleidoscope of colors as they spread their wings and flew off in directions.

"But how do you always know where we are?" Her eyes lit up. "Wait a minute—the MAP!"

He cocked his head and smiled. "Don't you have an important assignment?"

"Yes, but . . ."

He gently put his hand over her mouth. "Go complete your mission!"

CHAPTER 27

HOUSE OF PEACE?

Inspired by Sir Sean's timely appearance, Jazzi was filled with a new sense of hope. She was confident that finding peace would keep her from flunking out of school and bring her family back together. Waves of optimism flooded her soul as she and her committee hurried off.

"Now I know we're going to have our answer soon," she said, her face glowing.

"Hey, Jazzee, mon," Jamal asked, "wasn't dat de pirate dude who saved de Ox, mon?"

"What? I thought it was the soldier who saved Hakim," Ojitos jumped in.

"Nah, I'm pretty sure it was the same man who gave me the shovel," said Finn.

"He does look curiously familiar," Su agreed.

'Enery nodded along with Rachele and Kristina.

"Very observant." Oxford lowered his glasses and peeked over the rim. Jazzi looked at everyone and smiled. "We'll discuss him later. Right now we've got work to do!"

Excitement mounted as the group dashed up the stairs to the United Nations building, but when a security guard started yelling at them from down the hall, their plans were quickly thwarted."

"Oh no," Jazzi groaned. "It's one thing after another."

One by one, the kids looked at each other and hung their heads, discouraged. Time was running out and this was their only chance.

"Wait, Jazzi, I've got an idea," Ojitos piped up. "I'll stay behind and try to distract the guard while you and the others slip past him when he's not looking."

"Okay," she agreed. "What have we got to lose?"

The committee stood off to the side while Ojitos approached the guard.

"Hello, sir, I'm Ojitos." The man gave a polite nod. "I was just wondering . . . well, actually…it may be I'm more curious than simply wondering, but then again, it's probably a little of both . . ." The guard stared, confused. "Okay, I'll just come out and say it. Don't you get super bored just having to stand around here all day in the same place and stare at the same walls and ask the same questions because, man, I know I would and even though you probably meet some pretty cool peeps . . ."

As Ojitos continued chattering away, Jazzi and the others crept quietly past them. Once they had safely rounded the corner, they picked up the pace and went barreling into the lobby. Jazzi promptly collided with a stern-looking lady touting a sour expression on her face. She looked her up and down, grinning sheepishly.

"May I help you?" the woman asked, scowling as she peeled the young intruder off.

"Oh, uhhh . . ." Jazzi stammered as she stepped back. "I was just. . ."

Further conversation was crushed when Ojitos suddenly rounded the corner as if he were sliding into home plate.

"We did it!" he panted, out of breath. "I wasn't sure how much longer I was going to be able to keep that guard's attention." He reached up and gave Skawt a high five.

"You be da chatter master, mon." Jamal and Da Boyz exploded with silly smirks.

Ojitos, finally noticing the lady with the unfriendly stare, slowly shrank back. "Oops." He grinned. "Heh, heh—sorry!"

"Uh, yeah—um, he's with us." Jazzi smiled nervously. "You see, ma'am, we've traveled all the way around the world to get here." She stopped and cleared her throat. "We have a very important issue we need to address with the delegates. Would you be so kind to show us where they are meeting?"

"Issue?" The woman frowned down at her. "And you are?"

"We're the Kids' Worldwide Peace Club and we have peace issues." Jazzi replied openly.

"Hmmm, don't we all," the woman remarked. "Wait here please." She jotted down something on a piece of paper, then spun away down the hall.

Jazzi's stomach flip-flopped and she became filled with an overwhelming sense of fear. She looked outside the window: the sun was almost beginning to set. *We couldn't have come this far only to be turned away.*

A few moments later the woman returned and motioned to the kids.

"Come this way." Her face softened and there was a hint of a smile tugging at the corner of her lips. "I understand you know one of our delegates."

"Uhhh . . ." Jazzi looked at the woman, perplexed.

"Sir Sean?" The woman smiled. "I see your kids' club listed by his name."

Jazzi's eyes sparkled. "Sir Sean? Yes, of course! I've known Sir Sean for practically forever." She twirled around looking for nods of approval. The kids smiled in support.

"Then please, follow me," she said, and then stopped. She looked down at Nelson and Cat-Man-Doo then back up at Jazzi. "No animals allowed."

"Sure." Jazzi said politely.

The group nodded in unison.

Yes, we're in! Jazzi murmured under her breath as she ushered Nelson and Cat-Man-Doo to a comfortable corner to curl up.

The woman guided them down a long hall through a set of large glass doors and into an enormous meeting room. Dozens of delegates from around the world sat in a semicircle—a large wooden podium stood in the middle. All eyes were on the kids as they marched single file into the room.

"Oh—my—gosh!" Jazzi felt her confidence ebbing away at the sight of so many important people. Public speaking had never been her forte.

Oxford was sporting his usual 'I'm-about-to-hurl' face.

The United Nations chairman banged his gavel on his desk. He was a rather sober-looking gentleman with a full head of silver hair, which in Jazzi's opinion, nicely complemented his gray designer suit.

"We have a limited amount of time left today," he began, "so there will be no interruptions. I have been handed a request to grant these young people a special hearing. Therefore, let's get started." He turned toward the kids. "Who is your spokesperson?"

Nervously, Jazzi stepped forward, her heart pounding like the wings of Sir Sean's birds.

"Please begin, Miss . . ." He rustled through his papers. "I don't seem to have your name."

"Oh, that's okay, sir," she squeaked. "It's Jazzi, er, I mean, Imo Gene Hopkins."

Oxford flinched. She didn't sound like her confident old self.

"Go ahead, Miss Hopkins, or do you prefer Jazzi?"

"Jazzi is fine, your Honor."

"You'll have to speak louder."

"Yes, sir." She took a deep breath and glanced over at Oxford for support. He nodded and gave her a wink. To combat her fears, she imagined herself as an attorney in a court of law. She stood bold and confident, ready to present her opening paragraph. But, when she opened her mouth, a sudden rush of words spilled from her lips.

"You see, Mr. Chairman, it all began with a homework assignment that Mr. Shawnly . . ."

"Mr. Shawnly?" the chairman interrupted.

Oxford stepped forward. "He's our sixth grade teacher, your Honor." Then he politely stepped back.

The chairman nodded in acknowledgment. "Thank you. Please continue, Miss Jazzi."

"Okay, so anyways, Mr. Shawnly is the one who assigned this class project to define peace because it's an international requirement for all sixth grade students, and as you know, peace is a heavy topic and we didn't have a clue where to begin, but then we came up with an idea—well actually it was Oxy's idea…"

"Who's Oxy?" the chairman questioned, hitting the desk with his gavel.

Oxford raised his hand and motioned with a slight wave. The chairman harrumphed, and Jazzi continued her monologue in double time.

"…so, as I was saying, Oxy had this idea to develop a website that would connect us with kids from all over the world so we could pick their brains about peace and stuff." Her sentences began to run together. "I mean, hey, why not, because well, they might know something we don't, so we compiled a list of students' names and sent out an e-mail blast and that's how the Kids' Worldwide Peace Club began but…," she tapped her finger on her chin, "…I guess that was really only the beginning…"

"Beginning?" The chairman's eyes widened.

The audience watched fascinated by the speed with which Jazzi delivered this information. It was like she was in another dimension.

"…yes because we had no idea how huge this would actually become." Jazzi paused to take a breath. "Then we met Su on the beach when he climbed out from a hole in the sand…"

"Su? Hole in the sand?" The chairman scratched his head bewildered.

Su tipped his head so he would be noticed.

"That's Su nodding his head," said Jazzi, "and, I know what you're thinking because we had a hard time believing his *'hole in the sand story*' too—but then he showed us! We saw the CyberCoaster and the underground tunnels, and well—as you can imagine—that changed everything!"

"Yes," the chairman crossed his arms and leaned back in his chair, "I can only imagine."

"Excuse me!" One of the delegates called out. Jazzi stopped midsentence, her rhythm momentarily disrupted.

"What do you mean underground tunnels?" he asked. "And what in the world is a CyberCoaster?"

Jazzi resumed her speech. "Well, sir, a CyberCoaster is sort of a high-tech roller coaster thingy that travels through underground tunnels in cyber-time. Su will have to explain cyber-time because I still haven't figured that one out, but the CyberCoaster is how we were able to commute to other countries so fast." She let out a nervous giggle. "You wouldn't believe all the things that happened to us!"

"This is nonsense!" growled an angry delegate from the back of the room. "What does this have to do with anything? If we've assembled this meeting to discuss a silly homework assignment, then I'm leaving!"

And with that the rude delegate stood and picked up his briefcase. The committee of kids watched him intently. He didn't fit in with the other delegates. Something about him made Jazzi uneasy. She couldn't help staring. He was dressed from head-to-toe in black and had a skinny dark mustache that accented his small beady eyes. He reminded her of a villain from an old cartoon series.

"What's with Mr. Gloomy?" Jazzi said quietly to Oxford.

Oxford merely shrugged his shoulders, preoccupied with the whole situation.

Mr. Gloomy scowled at the other delegates. "Am I the only one who finds this a complete waste of time?" His voice was cold and distant.

The delegates began to speak softly amongst themselves. Jazzi felt her credibility slipping away. She took another step forward and found her voice again.

"Please," she pleaded, "don't leave!" She anxiously shoved her hand in her pocket and pulled out the map she had been guarding so carefully. She turned it over and read the message Sir Sean had scribbled on the back: *You are here. Speak from your heart.* Instantly, the words came to her and she knew what she needed to say.

"Excuse me!" she called out. "Peace affects all of us."

The delegates stopped murmuring and settled back in their seats.

"Carry on, miss," the chairman said, taking a drink of water.

"Your Honor," Jazzi's eyes were filled with hope, "since the United Nations is called 'The House of Peace,' our committee thought you would have all the answers." She smiled cheerfully. "That's why we came here."

The chairman choked as he downed his second gulp of water, spitting it all over his desk.

Oxford immediately stepped forward, concerned: "Do you need me to perform the Heimlich, sir? I'm certified in lifesaving techniques."

The chairman shook his head vigorously. He pounded his chest and finally caught his breath.

"No, no thank you," he coughed.

Then he peered down at Jazzi. "And what makes you think, young lady, that we would have any more answers to this question than you?"

CHAPTER 28
FLASHBACK TO REALITY

W ell, I thought . . ." Jazzi stammered as she stared back at him in disbelief, "I thought you were the experts because you *are* the House of Peace—aren't you? I mean, isn't that your job, isn't that what you do every day? We were counting on you because we're just a bunch of kids trying to complete a homework assignment." She hung her head deep in thought. Her fingers began to tremble as she looked down at the map again.

"Maybe there isn't just one easy answer, your Honor." The kids watched Jazzi without making a sound. Even Oxford seemed at a loss for words.

Mr. Gloomy did an about-face and stormed up to the podium. His forehead was furrowed, and his back was slightly bent as he leaned forward to speak. "It's obvious none of you has a clue about peace." He was practically spitting out his words, as he glared down at Jazzi with his icy-cold eyes. "PEACE IS AN ILLUSION!" he yelled. The words erupted from his mouth with such volcanic force that she thought surely he was about to transform into some hideous molten creature.

She took a deep breath, placed her hands on her hips, and declared bravely, "No disrespect, sir, but I think you're wrong." She stood her ground. "There has to be an answer because we traveled all this way to . . ."

"SILENCE!" he lashed back.

She took a step back and cupped her hands over her ears, trying to block out his angry words. His voice sent chills up her spine. No one dared move—even the chairman remained silent. All eyes were on Jazzi as Mr. Gloomy stood towering over her. He stared deep down into her eyes. She stared back, almost hypnotized. Then, like magic, a light went on inside her head. All at once Jazzi could see her own anger coming through him. She flashbacked to her bickering parents; the mean bullies at school; the cantankerous little crab; the tunnel of nasty rats; the disturbed snowman; the slithering snake; the tattooed banditos; the angry young soldiers—and then miraculously—the answer came...

"*Forgive*—that's it! A sense of peace began to well up inside of her pushing out all the anger and bitterness that had held her captive for so long. She took a deep breath and whirled around toward Skawt.

"You tried to tell me, didn't you?"

A big grin spread across his face. "Totally, but you had to discover it for yourself!"

Jazzi wasn't afraid anymore. She turned and faced the intimidating Mr. Gloomy. "Peace *is* possible, sir—it begins in your heart."

"WHAT?" he exploded.

"What I'm trying to say is, when your heart is full of anger, there's no room for peace!"

"WHY YOU LITTLE..." The delegate had reached his boiling point and in a fit of rage, lunged for Jazzi. Jamal and Da Boyz immediately jumped to her rescue and, with outstretched arms, joined hands and trapped Mr. Gloomy inside their circle.

"OUT OF MY WAY!" he cried out, pushing and shoving. He demanded they let him loose, but no one budged.

Jazzi wasn't about to give up. She could relate with Mr. Gloomy's anger and wanted, more than anything, to try to convince him. She leaned in closer. "When I saw the anger in your eyes, sir, I saw myself and…" her voice cracked, "it was ugly!"

"UGLY? I'll show you ugly!" Jazzi stumbled back in shock when the incensed delegate swung his briefcase as hard as he could at Jamal. Jamal was quick to duck, causing the briefcase to swing back around with such force, it hit Mr. Gloomy in his own head. "OWW!" He wailed and covered his face, but no one paid any attention to his outlandish display—all eyes were on Jazzi.

A hush fell over the audience as her eyes circled the room examining all the faces that were representing the different countries and cultures. *Wow*, she reflected inwardly, *I never realized our world was so colorful…*

"Make your point, young lady," the chairman insisted, tapping his finger on the edge of his desk.

"Yes, sir." She gathered her composure and stepped up to the podium, eyes shining hopefully. "I think before we can have peace—we must learn how to forgive."

The silence was deafening. Her eyes stared up at the ceiling as she mentally prepared her next words. "Okay, I admit I thought it was dumb at first, but now it totally makes sense. It kinda boils down to two things: forgive or be angry." There was no response. "Trust me people, being angry doesn't work—I know." She paced back and forth across the room wondering if she had said too much. She was just a kid, after all—why should anyone listen to her?

"Have you finished, Miss Jazzi?" The chairman's tone was considerably kinder.

"Almost," she confessed, "but, if it's okay, I do have one more thing."

The chairman looked at his watch and nodded. "We have a little time remaining."

Jazzi brushed back a curl that had fallen over her eye. "So I'm thinking," she took a deep breath, "I'm thinking we need to get over ourselves. You know—accept people for who they are. It's wrong to judge someone just because they think or believe different. I know I want to be myself—make my own choices—pick my *own* jeans…," she ran her hands down the sides of her legs, remembering the near riot that almost broke out over a pair of lederhosen. "Don't you?"

Several delegates nodded in agreement, while others shifted in their seats uncomfortably.

"Your Honor...," Jazzi became suddenly aware of how fragile she was, "what happened to me is a metaphor for what happens everywhere in the world. Skawt's not a weirdo, I think he's on to something."

The chairman leaned forward, his forehead puckered. "Skawt?"

Skawt signaled the chairman with a peace sign.

Jazzi walked over to Mr. Gloomy, she could see the sweat gushing from his pores as he struggled to free himself. She looked him directly in the eyes and said humbly, "It's easier to forgive than to fight."

Mr. Gloomy grabbed his chest, gasping, "You want ME to FORGIVE?" He became so outraged his face turned a bright crimson red and he began to puff up like a giant overinflated beach ball. The angrier he got, the bigger he grew. He became so bloated that his chubby fingers couldn't hold onto his briefcase, and with a grueling howl, he dropped to the floor.

Shocked by his outlandish behavior, one of the delegates got up and walked over to Jazzi. "You do make a point, young lady."

She heaved a big sigh. "Anger hurts the one who is angry more than the one it's meant to hurt."

Her eyes remained fixed on Mr. Gloomy as he rolled about the floor like a spoiled child throwing a temper tantrum. Sadly, he had made his choice and—as with every choice—there were consequences.

The kids' club, along with several other delegates, began to gather around Jazzi. One of the members said jokingly, "I make the motion we wear jeans every Friday to remind us of the valuable lesson these kids' have brought to us today!"

"I second the motion!" A delegate in the back of the room stood up applauding, followed by a string of others.

A slight snicker slipped out of the chairman's mouth as he raised his gavel. He was just about to bang it on the podium when a loud crashing sound vibrated through the building—shattered glass flew everywhere! A cloud of birds swarmed into the room and swooped down over Mr. Gloomy like he was fresh roadkill. Terror stricken, he crawled to his knees and flung his arms about, hoping to scare them away. Unfortunately, one very large bird was able to hook its talons into the back of his suit

coat and, in a flash, he was scooped off the floor and flying high above everyone's head.

The birds circled the room several more times before making their departure back through the broken window. On the way out, one of the birds became so irritated with Mr. Gloomy's endless ranting and raving, it poked him with its beak. To everyone's surprise, he popped open like an overfilled water balloon. Waves of water poured down on Jazzi, knocking her to the ground and soaking everything in sight. She lay sprawled out on the floor unconscious—strange thoughts and hazy images danced in her head. As the last rays of sunlight trickled into the room, she was mysteriously transported back to reality—back to a warm, sunny place—her favorite place to escape…

Jazzi's eyes burst open from the shock of the cold ocean water rushing in all around her—sand crabs tickled her toes in the oncoming tide. She looked up at Nelson and Oxford confused as they stood hovering over her.

"Jazzi—JAZZI?" Oxford gently shook her.

"Huh?" she moaned, rubbing her eyes.

"Are you okay?" Oxford pushed away a clump of wet curls stuck to her face. "I've been so worried. I thought we lost you!"

"Lost me?" Jazzi coughed up a mouthful of saltwater. "Where am I?" She squinted up at Oxford. "Have I been dreaming?"

"Dreaming? Are you kidding? That wave thrashed you. It's a miracle you're alive! You could have been history!" He rolled his head back.

"History? I hate history."

"I know, that's not what I meant. I'm just glad you're gonna live long enough to turn in your homework assignment."

"Oh that," she groaned. "I was trying to forget."

"Yeah, well, how fortunate for you I didn't."

"What do you mean?"

"While you were off self-destructing in the waves, I got the Kids' Worldwide Peace Club website up and running. We've had hits from places you would never imagine. One from a boy named Abraham who lives in Israel; one from a kid named 'Enery in England; there are two sisters from Holland, and—oh yeah—Ojitos from Mexico, and…"

"Su from China?" Jazzi cut in.

"Yeah and a boy from Iraq, and—wait! How do you know about Su?" Oxford asked.

"I dreamed it?" She giggled nervously and held out her hand. "A little help please?"

Oxford grabbed Jazzi's arm and pulled her to her feet. "So when do you want to get started? We have tons of e-mails from all over the world that really need to be answered as quickly as possible."

"Hey, I can barely stand up right now and you want me to start emailing kids I don't even know?" She grabbed a handful of curls and began to wring out the saltwater. "Don't you want to hear about my dream first?"

Oxford shook his head. "One of your dreams, Jazzi? No offense, but think I'll pass." He snapped his notepad shut.

"All I want to hear is a fork hitting my plate."

"Okay, I forgive you," she laughed jokingly. She bent down and pulled a pair of dry jeans from her backpack, then slid one leg in.

"Forgive me?" Oxford shrugged, "Thanks—I guess." He didn't have a clue what Jazzi was talking about. "Don't forget about our assignment!" He waved goodbye, then headed down the beach for home.

"Forget? How can I?" she shouted back. "You won't let me!"

Oxford waved his iNo in the air and laughed. She was right.

"Hey, Oxy?" she yelled. "You like my jeans?"

"They're fine, I guess—why?"

"Just wondered." Jazzi grinned because, at that very moment, she didn't care if Oxford liked her jeans or not. It was her own unique style and that's all that mattered. She picked up her backpack, slung it over her shoulder, and whistled for Nelson.

Then, oddly, Jazzi heard a familiar sound. It was a mysterious sound—a kind of whisking, whirring sound. She whirled around in astonishment.

Hmmm, that's strange, she thought. *I know I've heard that sound before. Oh well, me and my imagination.*

"Nelson!" Jazzi whistled and called out his name. After several minutes had passed, she spotted a rooster-tail of sand flying up in the air and figured it had to be him. She whistled again and, reluctantly, he came trotting over.

"I think we've had enough excitement for one day—don't you, boy?" She reached down and patted his head tenderly. Nelson looked back at the spot where he had been digging and let out several friendly barks. As he tagged along behind Jazzi, he would stop every so often and look back—it was odd, as if he sensed something…

THREE WEEKS LATER

Jazzi sat at her desk paralyzed with fear. Today was the day Mr. Shawnly was handing back the peace essays. She squeezed her eyes shut and clenched the desk with both hands, bracing herself for the worst. Then, slowly, she opened one eye and peeked up at him—he stood towering above her. He leaned over and passed her the paper then moved down the row to the next student. Her hand trembled as she nervously unfolded the paper and read the grade.

"An A—really?" Her mouth dropped open. "YESSS!" She sat up proudly in her seat—corkscrew curls draped over her shoulders, framing the back of her chair.

Oxford was sitting at his desk behind her. He reached over and planted a friendly punch on her shoulder. "See, Jazzi? Things really *are* possible when you believe."

She smiled, contented. She could hardly wait to tell her parents!

"So, Jazzi, looks like phase one is completed," Oxford said with a smile and thumbs-up.

"Phase one?"

"Uh yeah, phase one of the Kids' Worldwide Peace Club project—remember? We still have all those global e-mails and other countries to explore. This is just the beginning!" He grinned from ear to ear.

"Sure, it's at the top of my 'to do' list." Jazzi ran her fingers through her curls trying to tame them as she turned towards Oxford. "Hey—you look *okay* today." She batted her eyelashes.

"I do?" He perked up, surprised. "You mean it?"

"Uh-huh, you might even be the next trendsetter." She leaned over and gave him a kiss on the cheek. He blushed until his face matched the color of his hair.

"Good work students!" Mr. Shawnly spoke like a proud teacher as he stood in front of the class. "And a special high-five to Jazzi for taking the assignment seriously."

Several students laughed, while others cheered. Jazzi blushed and glanced out the window. She was just in time to see her dad's car pulling up in front of the school. As he got out and stretched his long legs, she felt a sudden rush of love.

Maybe this wasn't such a dumb assignment after all! With a contented sigh, Jazzi closed her eyes, anxious to begin the next adventure. But before she had a chance to drift away, Mr. Shawnly strolled over to her desk. As he looked down at her with an encouraging wink—she couldn't help but notice a certain familiarity about his twinkling blue eyes…

A SPECIAL THANKS

I thank God for putting this story in my heart and giving me the strength to persevere through many teeter-tottering years as it came to fruition. I'm also grateful for my husband, David, who has been both loving and patient during the whole process. Without him I never would have made it to the finish line. My heartfelt thanks goes out to my son, Sean, for not only inspiring me, but for adding his creative input throughout the entire story. I also owe so much to my dear friend and mentor, Richard, who encouraged my imagination to write. Had he not come into my life this adventure series would never have been born.

My deepest gratitude goes to my beautiful children, Christopher, Cassandra, and Sean. You are my presents from God who have each, in your own special way, helped me unwrap the lessons in this book—how to love and forgive. I also thank my amazing stepsons, Kevin and Scott, and my precious grandchildren, Rachele, Lauren, Kristina, Trent, Raquel, and my new great grandson, JJ. You are light in a dark world, and it is because of your prayers and faith in me, along with my wonderful friends, that I can now say with greater conviction: all things are possible to those who believe.

ABOUT THE AUTHOR

Gayle Johnston Arlich, a first-time author born in Los Angeles, claims she had a reawakening at the age of fifty. That is when she discovered her love for writing. As her five grandchildren put it, she's not only Grammy Gayle, an artist who can "paint with paint," she's an artist who can "paint with words."

Throughout her life as a mother, teacher, and career woman, Gayle has spent many hours teaching kids and volunteering her talents to work with youth organizations through schools and worthwhile charities. She has always had a heart for "tweeners," knowing the challenges they face, and so her book themes evolved. She has a unique way of expressing her imagination as she addresses teen challenges, and you will be both captivated and entertained once you step aboard the magical CyberCoaster. Please join Jazzi G and her quirky friends as they *Search for the Missing Peace*, the first book in the Adventures of Jazzi G series.

Jazzi G Industries

P.O. Box 877

San Marcos, CA 92079

Phone: (760) 481-9616

Email: Gayle@Jazzi-G.com

Jazzigbook.com

CPSIA information can be obtained at www.ICGtesting.com
Printed in the USA
LVOW08s0028050816

499038LV00001B/1/P